Healing His Soul's Mate

Wiccan Haus Book 13

By
Dominique Eastwick

Copyright © 2016 by Dominique Eastwick
ISBN: 978-1-68361-029-8
Cover art by Fiona Jayde

Published by Decadent Publishing Company, LLC
Look for us online at:
www.decadentpublishing.com

~A Note from the Author~

Finally we get to see Dana give birth, thank you to all the fan who stuck with us through the change of publishers and for the Wiccan Haus what feels like a rebirth.

http://dominiqueeastwick.blogspot.com/p/contact-me.html

Dedication

Dedicated to Decadent Publishing, Kate, Val and Lisa for giving Wiccan Haus a new home and loving it as much as I do. Only fitting that the rebirth of the series is a birth story.

Welcome to the Wiccan Haus

Something wiccan this way comes to a mystical mysterious island where authors get to play and bring their love stories to life. At the Wiccan Haus you will meet Rekkus, Cyrus, Sage, Sarka, Cemil and Myron, all of whom return in most if not all the stories. Yes each one will eventually get their HEA as well.

We hope you enjoy the stories from all the authors and return time and again to keep up with the staff and meet new characters along the way. But fear not if this is your first or twenty-first story each book stands on its own..

Prologue

"**O**h no!" Myron flicked the cards on the receptionist desk again. Pushing her purple hair behind her ear she glanced at the old grainy cuckoo clock on the far wall. "Not happening—this cannot be happening now."

Cyrus, having watched the gypsy, fascinated by her confusion, for the last five minutes, came to his feet, "What can't be happening now, beautiful?"

He placed his gloved hand on her shoulder, leaning in close to look at the cards as if this time he would see what she did in the random placement of the numbers and face cards. Still, he viewed a strange game of solitaire laid before them. But he knew whatever she saw, he needed to listen. Myron and her cards were often the voice of reason on the island.

"Has Dana knotted something on her body again?" he asked with some levity. For the last seven weeks, their Romney receptionist had carried a pair of scissors everywhere in superstitious belief the very pregnant Dana could harm her unborn child by tying anything around her body. The gypsy cut off any knot on the other woman's clothes. And, as most maternity clothes had some sort of tie, most of Dana's clothes had been mutilated by Myron and her scissors.

"Do not mock me. Knots are bad luck. We do not want the umbilical cord to have a knot in it."

Cyrus decided this might not be the time to reawaken the debate about some cultures believing knots in umbilical cords good luck. "I am not mocking, luv."

Myron's violet eyes were full of worry before she reached into the tapestry carpetbag beside her. After a minute of rummaging, she brought out her grandmother's aged deck. Cyrus stayed her from removing them from their fragile box. In a voice intended for only Myron to hear but brooking no argument, he asked, "Why, by the goddess, do you need Babba's old deck? What have you seen?"

Myron's hand shook under his. Her voice almost trance-like, she said, "Dana," repeating the name with each card in the spread.

"What about Dana?" If they weren't so used to Rekkus sneaking up on them, they might have jumped out of their skins. The were-tiger more than anyone would want to figure out why his mate's name lay on the gypsy's lips.

"The cards are dark. They hum, but something is preventing them from getting the information they need."

"What could prevent the information from being received?" Rekkus asked. "But they are reading Dana?"

"Give her a second, Rek." Cyrus addressed his best friend but never turned to him, focused on keeping Myron calm.

"Family," she announced and repeated the two

words, Dana and family, over and over as she laid the cards down faster and faster.

"Damn it, is she in danger?" Rekkus' voice broke with the intensity of his concern.

"Dana family. Dana family arriving." The cards stopped.

"The cubs?" Rekkus asked.

"Did you say cubs?" Cyrus turned on his friend. "As in more than one baby?"

Myron shook her head. "No, the babies are fine, and it's not their time."

"You did say cubs. Myron you knew? She knew?" Cyrus demanded of the two of them. Damn it why had no one told him Dana was having twins.

"Of course I knew." She flicked a card on his hand, a card he suspected might be the joker.

Rekkus growled the inhuman growl that either brought people to attention or sent them running for cover. "Myron, what are the fucking cards saying?"

Cyrus stared at him, unable to believe he had directed his infamous temper at Myron. The silence lasted until Rekkus took a deep breath and pleaded, "Myron, please."

Rekkus spoke in grunts and growls and even put up with Myron's kitty jokes, tolerating her calling him Puss in Boots from time to time. But the big tiger—almost eight hundred pounds in tiger form—had never once begged for anything. Until now.

"Give me a second." Myron grabbed his hand and gave it a reassuring squeeze. Rekkus had lost so much more than Cyrus' family, but he never missed a step. The thought or hint of Dana in trouble, and the big guy crumpled.

The old deck Myron had inherited from her grandmother gave off a soft shuffling sound as she worked them over and over in her hands. Lifting her face to Rekkus, she laid three cards face up.

"Dana," Rekkus said.

She nodded. "Dana." Then she positioned three more down on top of the others, horizontal this time. "Family."

Sarka threw open her office door behind Myron's desk. "The ferry is coming through the fog wall at this very minute. What the hell is everyone doing hanging around here, goofing off, and not down at the dock where you are supposed to be?"

Cyrus looked out the open doors of the lobby toward the walkway heading down to the eastern dock then focused on the cards laid out on the reception desk. Myron laid down three more cards.

"Here!" Myron threw her cards on the table as the ferry tooted its horn, emerging from the fog wall. "Dana's sister is dealing with emotional damage and needs healing. She's on the ferry with her parents!"

The room, hell, the Haus, fell eerily silent, as if the building didn't dare creak.

"How the hell did Dana's relatives get a reservation, let alone get on the ferry without me being told?" Rekkus demanded, fist clenched at his side.

"Welcome back, moody kitty," Myron muttered.

Rekkus slammed a fist into the counter, scattering the cards and cracking the marble. "Myron!"

"Rekkus!" Sarka shrieked.

"I didn't take the reservation." Myron crossed her arms. "If you think for a second I would allow those people—"

"Someone had to accept their reservations."

Cyrus didn't want to add to the hostility, but Rekkus had a good point, even if he didn't express it well.

"Would someone tell me what the hell is going on?" Sarka, never one to be ignored, stood, hands on her hips.

"Sarka, mind your own fucking business," Rekkus growled.

The O forming on Sarka's face made Myron giggle and Cyrus would have laughed, too, if the situation wasn't growing precarious. His friend's golden eyes glowed with para rage. Who could blame him? The way his in-laws had treated his mate had cemented the tiger's hostility toward them.

"Rek, listen." Cyrus called on the calming powers of his sister Sage to help him say the right thing. And where the hell was Sage? If ever they needed her, it was now. "It doesn't matter how they got the reservations. In less than fifteen minutes, they will be here, and it might be best if Dana heard the news from you. Not that you seem big on sharing any news these days with, say, me. Something important like there being two babies instead of one. Things the godfather might want to know about."

"For the love of the goddess, I didn't tell anyone." Rekkus turned on him. "Dana wanted something to stay private."

"Myron knew."

"Cards, Cyrus. The cards told me, and I don't read and tell." She grimaced. "Okay, I don't when someone asks me not to."

"Oh."

"With that cleared up, perhaps, Rekkus, you would like to go tell your mate," Myron said with a hesitant smile.

"Tell me what?"

Everyone turned to face the front door where a very pregnant Dana waddled in. Rekkus prowled around the receptionist desk toward his mate. Cyrus could've sworn the temperature rose five degrees as he neared. Before Rekkus reached Dana, Myron spoke up. "Kitty, I promise, should my cards read anything of concern, I will always tell you."

"Thank you, my chwaer." He led Dana to one of hundreds of chairs situated around the island for her comfort. "Dana...."

"I feel as if this is the longest pregnancy ever." She rubbed her belly with a sigh. Dana remained standing and glanced at Rekkus then the others waiting around the lobby. "Don't you have the ferry to meet?"

"About the ferry." Rekkus hesitated, a dead giveaway something was wrong.

"Rekkus, what is it?" She frowned at their worried faces. "Why is Sarka looking like I might lose it? For that matter, everyone."

"Dana, there's something I need to tell you about the ferry." Rekkus hesitated again, something Cyrus hadn't believed the were-tiger capable of. "There are some unwelcome passengers on the boat at the moment."

"Unwelcome, how?"

"For the love of the goddess. Dana, your mother, father, and sister have reservations here for the week," Sarka announced as if ripping a Band-Aid off. "There. It's out now. Can we move on?"

Dana paled and swayed. "Why were they allowed to make a reservation? Rekkus? I don't want them here. Not now."

"We don't know, but I am going to find out."

Rekkus pulled his mate close and wrapped his arms around her. "Myron...."

She put up a hand. "I swear it wasn't me."

"Well, I wouldn't have a clue how to log them into the system." Hell, the last time Cyrus had turned on the computer it had crashed.

Only one person hadn't denied responsibility.

Sarka stood defiant, not moving. "Fine, I might have taken the reservation."

Cyrus had heard Rekkus growl before. He had seen him angry enough to tear a man or paranormal limb from limb. He watched Rekkus dive into the water to destroy a were-shark who'd hurt his mate. Rekkus turned on Sarka and growled like nothing any of them had ever heard before. The temperature dropped twenty degrees in a matter of seconds as he hurdled the desk.

Cyrus moved between them, and Sarka took a step back, but Rekkus reached over his shoulder and pinned Sarka by the neck to the wall. His chest heaved. The fact he had not ripped out Sarka's throat told more about his self-control than anything else.

"Rek, my friend, you need to release my sister."

"I could kill you for what you have done," Rekkus growled but loosened his grip. He didn't move other than to withdraw his hand.

Cyrus put his arm out as if doing so would protect her, and without turning to her he said, "Sarka, in the office now."

"Do as he said." Cemil rounded the corner in a run. His voice held a nervousness which belied the fact Sarka may have crossed the line this time.

But, in true Sarka fashion, she defied any order. "How dare he? I will not—"

"You will do as I say and do it now." Cemil's

voice brooked no argument as he went over and pulled Dana toward her mate. "Dana, I need you to control your man."

Dana stumbled and Cyrus prayed it wouldn't set Rekkus off. She righted herself and approached. "How?"

How indeed because it wouldn't take much for Rekkus to get through him or the door to tear his sister to shreds.

Cemil's voice calm and light said, "Have Rekkus touch your belly. I need you to talk him down before he shifts."

Dana squinted at Cemil as if she had been in a trance, and perhaps she had been, but Dana was aware of the electricity her mate put off. So far, he remained in human form, for had he shifted, not one person or security guard on the island could've stopped him. Hurt a shifter's mate and no law could protect you.

"Rekkus, please." Dana's voice cracked as she moved his hand over her extended abdomen and reached up to kiss his cheek. As he turned toward her, his shoulders relaxed.

Cyrus released the air he had pent up and gave Dana a reassuring nod.

"We will deal with this issue together. But I can't do it alone. I need you to be strong for me." She scanned the room. "I need everyone here to be strong because you are my family, not the three people on the boat who disowned me."

Cyrus took the other side of Dana, and, placing one of her hands in his, he squeezed. "Cemil, you'll deal with our sister? Make sure she understands if I ever catch her doing this again, she will have to deal with me, because if it's between losing Rekkus and Dana over stuff like this, I will vote her off the fucking island."

Cemil nodded and this time he did not walk on air. He stormed into the office, slamming the door and closing him and Sarka into the small room. She'd stepped over the line this time. Cyrus didn't know if Cemil's emotions got the better of him because Rekkus' emotions were so volatile or perhaps he was as sick of Sarka's bull as everyone else.

Dana broke the silence. "Shall we go greet the Stones?"

"Together," Rekkus said.

Cyrus squeezed Dana's hand again, and Myron gripped her shoulders, all of them infusing her with their strength. "Together," Cyrus agreed. No one was going to hurt his family again.

No one!

Chapter One

Three weeks earlier, New York City

Ashlynn Stone bit her lip as her nerves got the better of her. The kindhearted nurse stood above her, she wondered if she had the courage to go through with this.

"Ms. Stone, are you sure you're ready to see the scars?"

"No, but sometimes our imagination is worse." She accepted the mirror from the nurse and closed her eyes. Brave words, but she would never be ready. With shaking hands, she raised the mirror and let out a cry. She traced the scar above her left eyebrow moving down to the place below her ear on her neck.

She returned the mirror with a thank you and laid her head back on the white hospital pillowcase. The plastic surgery had done little to hide the ugly and ragged mark. Her career as a model was over, and any hope she had lay like those bandages on the floor. The headaches kept her up at night with such pain it split her head in two. Hurt so fierce she thought she would die from it. To hell with a career built on fake beauty. What she wouldn't give for some inner peace.

The nurse touched her arm. "Bad luck the light falling from the truss."

"Indeed." What else could she say? At least this nurse hadn't mouthed platitudes, saying it would heal, or it didn't look so bad. At least she hadn't lied to her. Because it was bad, but her beauty would've faded anyway, right?

So far, she was less upset about the loss of her career as a top model than she'd expected to be. Her mother seemed more devastated by the turn of events, but she always put a great deal of credit on appearance and name, and what a coup it had been to have a beautiful daughter to brag about. Her daughter the model. But now her mother could barely bring herself to look at her. In the last two weeks, she'd visited only once for a moment.

Her father, who had through her life always been less hands-on, came every day, sitting with her for hours on end. He would come between his rounds to check on her and stay with her while she slept. For the first time in her life, she saw her father as a person, not only the top OB/GYN in New York or the society husband she'd always thought him to be.

The soft knock filled the room, and she flinched as the sounds bounced around inside her skull. The nurse frowned at her. "Shall I send them away?"

"I think it depends on who they are." She would prefer her mother went away, rather than rattle on about how much weight Ashlynn had put on or some top-notch surgeon she had found.

"Okay, but if you want me to get rid of them, just say your head hurts and you need your meds."

"Thank you."

"Jessie?" The last person she expected to see walk through the door was Jessie Ranata, her

11

estranged sister's best friend. As Dana had been disowned by her mother over a year ago in front of friends and family and had shown no interest of keeping in touch with anybody else, Jessie's visit shocked her. A small part of Ashlynn had expected Dana to call or show up. If anything would've brought her back, this should have, but having been on the receiving end of her mother's displeasure, Ashlynn had to acknowledge it sucked enough to send her running away.

"I hope it's all right. I thought about calling but chickened out. In the end, I figured a surprise might be best." Jessie glanced at the nurse before walking in, her voice low as if mimicking the darkness of the room.

"Jessie, of course it's okay. I'm simply surprised."

A larger-than-life smile came over Jessie's face. She was weighed down with the shopping bags of a woman with too many credit cards and too much time on her hands. "I have to admit I have paced outside the hospital today for about an hour, wondering whether to come in or not. Then I spent another twenty minutes wandering the halls, wondering if I should enter your room."

"I'm glad you stopped in. It's nice to have visitors." Ashlynn watched as Jessie fought with the bags in her arms and then dropped them on the table across the room, a gigantic shopping bag with blue bears on it from one of the uptown baby boutiques on the top. "Someone's having a baby?"

Jessie paused. "You're joking right?"

"I saw the baby bag and wondered if you were...."

"No I'm not pregnant, I thought you.... It's Dana."

"Dana's pregnant!" Ashlynn screeched and regretted it as her head reverberated all the way to the base of her neck.

"I thought you knew." Jessie stood and reached for a wet cloth from the sink. "Headaches? This might help if I place it over your eyes. I promise not to stay long. I wanted to see if I could help. I never meant to make it worse."

"Does she know?" Ashlynn asked then clarified. "About my accident. I assume she knows she is preggers."

Jessie shook her head before laying the cloth over her brow. "Did you call her? Did anybody think to inform her?"

"The news played the damned video of the light falling on my head for days on end."

"Yes, well, The Wiccan Haus isn't known for its TV and Internet. Someone should have given her a call."

"Why would we call? She hasn't called us since she left, didn't even bother to tell us she got married until after the fact."

After a long silence, Jesse spoke. "I can't imagine she would've said anything to anyone after the way your mother disowned her."

"I didn't disown her." And she hadn't. She and her sister had never been close, but she wished they had been.

"No, but you didn't stand up for her either, so perhaps she found your silence agreement enough." Jessie flipped the wet cloth. "I shouldn't have come. I heard about the accident, and then I heard about the scar tissue and I thought I'd give you this." She fished something out her bag.

"What is it?" Ashlynn asked peeking around the

cloth.

"It's a cream. It might not help. It won't take away the scars, but it should soften them, make them less visible, less noticeable."

"What is in it?"

"Oh, don't open it yet, smells horrid but it works. Sage Rowan at the Wiccan Haus made this for me. There isn't a lot left, but if you want more, I'll ask her to make some."

"Thank you. That is kind. I wonder if she has something for these headaches."

"You might be surprised. Perhaps you should book a week or two there. When all else fails, they seem to be able to work miracles."

"That might not be such a bad idea." The deep voice of her father, Dr. Eugene Stone, pulled her attention back to the door which had opened without her noticing.

"Dad?"

"Have another headache, do you? Hello, Jessie, what a surprise."

Jessie fidgeted in her seat. "I wanted to stop in and see how she was doing and give her something."

His smile held sadness. "Very kind of you."

An awkward silence followed as Ashlynn wondered when Jessie would check her watch and make the inevitable is that the time? excuse. But it didn't happen, and after some time, her father said in a voice choked with emotion, "How is she?"

"Dana?" Jesse asked, her voice strained.

"Yes."

"You have to say her name if you want me to answer. You have to acknowledge she exists." Bitterness laced Jessie's comment.

Ashlynn's head hurt from the tension in the room, but she needed to know more about Dana's life than her marital status and intent never to come home again. Shock ran through her at the tears glistening in her dad's eyes.

Ever since the night Dana left her fiancé at the altar, nobody had spoken her name in their house. Even the day a courier delivered the exact amount of money spent for the wedding that never happened, no one talked about her. Almost as if Dana never existed.

"Is Dana all right. Is she happy? Does her husband treat her well? I don't even know his name." Dr. Stone rubbed a hand over his weary face.

Jessie's shoulders relaxed. "She's very happy, and Rekkus treats her like a princess. He adores her. His last name is hard to pronounce. Don't ask me to try, I can't, it's some old Welsh family name."

"This Rekkus, what does he do?" Her dad took a seat in the rolling chair at the foot of her bed. He inched closer to Jessie, waiting for information on his daughter.

"Officially, he is head of security for the Wiccan Haus, but I will eat my purse if he is simply a security guard. And, he isn't your run-of-the-mill mall cop. This guy screams Special Ops."

"You seem to like him," he noted, leaning forward.

"I do but I don't know him very well. He isn't a get-to-know-you kind of guy. I think he tolerated me because Dana wanted me there."

"Do you think she's happy?"

Jessie nodded. "I think you need to consider taking Ashlynn to the Wiccan Haus. You've tried every bit of modern medicine to help her. It's been in every paper on every newscast. I have seen them work miracles on the island, and Dana has talked about the amazing work they do. It would be worth a try."

"You think they can help?"

"I do, and what have you got to lose?"

"Feeling as she does about us, do you think she would even want us there?"

Jessie shrugged again but nodded. "There's only one way to find out. Make a reservation. If they accept it, then you go. If they say no, you have your answer."

"I did some research on the island when your sister decided to stay. They seem legitimate. I worried at first they were a cult who'd gotten their claws into her. But the more I read, the more impressed I became. I am very worried about these headaches, and if they can help, I think we need to try."

"Me, too, Dad." She took his hand and squeezed it. "There's something else. Jessie told me she's pregnant."

"Pregnant?"

"I don't think it's been an easy pregnancy, either. My last visit was at Rekkus' request, not Dana's. He thought a visit from me would cheer her up, and when you meet your son-in-law, you will understand why I am concerned."

"I'm not following."

Neither did Ashlynn, but she assumed her headache made it hard for her to follow the conversation.

"Rekkus, though he loves Dana, is not what you would call a people person. He would be quite happy to never have a single soul besides Dana and the

Rowans set foot on the island."

Chapter Two

The thick mist engulfed the ferry. Jessie had mentioned it, but until Ashlynn saw the wall with her own eyes, she hadn't grasped how immense a fog wall could be. A small amount of terror ran down her spine. It was something out of a horror film. Almost as if they would never return the same as they left.

The crew worked together without a single word being spoken. A pale woman no more than four and a half feet tall approached Ashlynn and handed her a set of big, obnoxious brown earphones. She pointed to her head. As the pressure in her skull increased so did comprehension. She put the ear protection on, and, for the first time in weeks, all pain receded.

The pressure in her skull eased, and a wave of exhaustion came over her. Fighting the pain had become so draining. She'd believed she would never be without it again. She relished the feeling of nothing and dreaded the return of normal. As the island came in sight, she removed the headset, overcome by the view in front.

"On my."

"Just you wait. This is nothing." A middle-aged woman with streaks of silver running through her black hair took a deep breath and smiled. "It gets better every time I come."

Her dad stood at the port side. "What do you think, Dad?"

"I think I can understand why your sister stayed." His smiled was edged with apprehension. After all, no one could guess how Dana would react to them. And having always been the golden child, Ashlynn had never bothered to understand the plight of her older sister. In fact, growing up, she would have done anything to remain the golden child. Now her mother did all the things she had done to her sister. She belittled the weight Ashlynn had packed on since the accident, ignoring the basic needs of the daughter she purported to love. Ashlynn had a glimpse of the hell Dana had experienced growing up. "Where's Mom?"

"Your mother is in a snit. She's in the dining area and refuses to come out. Perhaps informing her where we were going after the boat had sailed was not a good plan after all."

Ashlynn didn't understand her dad's need to have her mother come along at all, but perhaps if the people on this island could help with her headaches, it could help her mother as well.

A long, well-maintained dock came into view. Ashlynn walked to the bow of the ship and viewed the path leading to the hilltop. Before the enormous Bavarian building stood three forms. "I think that's Dana there, by the main building."

Her dad put an arm around her shoulders. "I wasn't sure they would know who we were. When I made the reservation, the curt woman didn't ask or allow me a second to say we were related to Dana."

"Perhaps Dana greets every boat." She gazed back up toward the three figures. The two men dwarfed her sister, made her look petite. A word no one in her house had ever used to describe Dana.

"Perhaps, or maybe she is meeting her demons head on."

At the sound of someone clearing their throat behind them, they turned to find one of the crew members. "Dr. Stone, your wife is refusing to disembark when we dock. Shall we ask security to escort her off? We are not heading directly back to the mainland, so she cannot stay on the boat."

He shook his head. "I will deal with my wife."

Ashlynn followed her dad into the cabin as the crew brought luggage up on deck in preparation for docking. They didn't need to deal with the diva woman as well. Although, looking at the well-muscled crew, she doubted they would have any problems dealing with anyone.

Their mother sat by a table. "Nancy, it's time to get ready. Come up on deck. The island is beautiful," her father said in a calm voice.

"I will be damned if I set foot on that hippy island." She stared past them. "They will take me back to the mainland immediately, or I'll go on every social network and make sure everyone hears how subpar this hotel is."

"You have two choices. You can move of your own volition or you can have security remove you. You can make a scene and have your daughter's husband order his men to deal with you."

"And Jessie said Rekkus would like nothing more than to embarrass you the way you have embarrassed

Dana," finding her voice, Ashlynn added.

"I embarrassed Dana." Turning on Ashlynn, her mother's screech echoed through Ashlynn's head causing her to grab it in pain.

"Nancy, enough. Ash and I will be disembarking. If you don't, I'll see to it every person on the ship chats with the press when we return if security has to remove you! I'm here to see if we can't amend our broken relationship with our daughter while healing the other. I don't need you to do this, my dear, whether you come on or don't, I don't care."

The boat bumped the edge of the dock, and Ashlynn grabbed the rail to stay upright.

Ashlynn murmured, "Mother, you coming?"

"I don't have much choice, do I? But I don't have to like it, and I certainly don't have to be polite to your sister. Dana is no daughter of mine. You might remember that as you collude with your father."

She wanted to say something to her mother about how Dana seemed happy enough without any of the Stones in her life. Ashlynn began to believe perhaps not having her mother in her life would make her happy as well, but she left it unsaid. Whatever she wanted to say wouldn't make a difference anyway, even if it would've left her mother openmouthed with shock. Seeing her mother speechless would've given her great joy, but in the end she did what she always did, she lowered her head and walked away. She joined her father, yet neither acknowledged her mother's presence behind them.

Her father picked up his bags and went to pick up Ashlynn's as well when a tall dark man stepped forward. The other man boarded as soon as the ramp had been attached to the ferry. His uniform connoisseur of a tight-fitting black T-shirt over what even Ashlynn had to admit was a well-cut body from his broad shoulders to his formfitting black jeans that left nothing to the imagination.

"Miss Stone, we will take your bags up to your room." He lifted the two bags as if they weighed no more than a feather pillow and threw them over his shoulders before he headed back off the dock, leaving Ashley with a weak smile. She hadn't packed much but carrying anything more than her purse hurt, and she didn't want her father having to carry it up for her. From behind, she could hear the sound of another security guard.

"Mrs. Stone must carry her own." She spun to see another security guard dressed in the same black uniform and combat boots.

Her mother bridled, unused to being ordered about. "I thought this was a top-notch resort. I will not carry my own bags like some peon."

"Every able-bodied guest carries their own bag. You are able-bodied, thus you can carry your own bag."

"Eugene, I thought you said this would be an exclusive, top-of-the-line resort."

"It is, but perhaps it's long past time you pull your own weight."

Ashlynn watched the man with her two bags pause partway up the hill to chat with the other men and her sister, who held the hand of a man who stood a good foot taller.

"If that's Rekkus," Dr. Stone said, "Jessie wasn't exaggerating."

They took the hill at a snail's pace, stopping face-to-face with a very pregnant Dana. To Ashlynn's shock, her dad dropped his bags and embraced his elder daughter, tears streaming down his face. Dana stood, arms at her side for a moment then threw them around their father, tears streaming down her face. The big man—must be Rekkus—hovered nearby, brows furrowed. The other man, tall with long blond hair, murmured, "They are tears of joy. Relax, Rekkus."

Her father pulled back only to re-embrace Dana tighter. "Dad, you need to share," Ashlynn said with the uncertain smile.

Their father stepped to the side seemingly too choked up to speak a word.

"Can you ever forgive me?" Ashlynn's words came out in quick succession.

Dana's brow furrowed. "Oh, Ash, for what?"

"For everything. For never standing up for you. For not stepping forward at the wedding." After Jessie left, Ash realized how life must have been for Dana. Her sister had never had it easy, and although Ashlynn could cast most of the blame on her mother, she had to bear some of the guilt as well.

Ashlynn found herself pulled into a loving embrace of her big sister, possibly the first time they had ever hugged. Their mother had never allowed any form of affection between the two. As far back as her earliest memories, the sisters had been kept apart. "You aren't to blame, but if it's forgiveness you need, you have it."

Tall, Dark, and Intimidating grunted, giving her a pointed stare.

Dana glared at him. "My forgiveness is mine to give. Your views on it are crystal clear."

"You are too forgiving," Rekkus said but, unlike Dana, he didn't bother to lower his voice.

What defense did she have to a statement of truth? After another brief hug, Ashlynn pulled back. "Dana, you're gorgeous. You're glowing."

Tears welled from deep within her. "I learned of your accident today. I am so sorry. I would've come to visit had I been made aware of the accident. Oh, where are my manners?" Dana reached behind her and pulled Rekkus forward. He grunted or maybe growled. It sounded like a growl, almost animalistic. "Rekkus, I want you to meet my father Dr. Eugene Stone...."

The distance between them and Rekkus she had no intention of crossing. He intimidated her, and she could sense his mistrust of them. In a formal, almost military voice, he greeted them. "Dr. Stone, welcome to the island."

"Please call me Eugene. Thank you for taking such good care of my daughter. I have great amends to make, and I hope we can get to know each other better while we are here."

"Dana would like that." Rekkus leaned back as another man came to whisper into his ear. He nodded in the direction of the boat. Following his line of sight, Ashlynn realized their mother hadn't followed.

"Dana, I think I should warn you...." Ashlynn began, but she wasn't really sure how or what to say. She was silently thankful when Dana reached out and touched her arm.

"It's about our mother. You don't need to warn me about anything. Some things will never change in this world. She is one of those things."

As much as she hated the way her mother treated the situation and Dana, she had to be thankful she didn't have to explain the nastiness. Even after all this time, her mother couldn't show a degree of motherhood toward Dana. Dana did what she always did. Showing compassion, she reached forward, grabbed Ashlynn's hand, and gave an understanding squeeze.

"Two out of three family members isn't bad, right?" Even though through the bravado, Ashlynn could see her emotions brimming. Her husband must've detected it because the gigantic man's arms wrapped around her.

"We can deal with her if you like," Rekkus said.

Dana looked over her shoulder at her husband. "Deal with her how?"

"I can either have someone cater to her demands or she can be treated like a regular guest." To Ashlynn's surprise, Rekkus' voice softened.

"And who would you have cater to her every need?"

"Oh, I think Telly would be the perfect choice, don't you?"

The man in the sunglasses and gloves groaned, but his lips switched. "Poor boy. One mistake will forever be his doom."

"Telly?" Ashlynn asked.

"He is a teenager who comes to the island once a month." Dana nudged the man in sunglasses. "Cyrus, please meet my father and my sister, Ashlynn. Dad, Ash, this is Cyrus Rowan and his brother Cemil. The Rowans own the Wiccan Haus."

Cemil, light and friendly, welcomed them both with open arms. He had an air of happiness from within, very carefree, but also exuded strength. Cyrus extended gloved hands for her father. His darkness relayed a deep sadness. Despite their differences, identical ice-blue eyes stared back at her.

"I say let her carry her own bags like a normal guest," Ashlynn mumbled, casting a glance back to the dock where their mother sat on her bags, refusing to move.

"The second group of arrivals are due here, and we need to get her settled. I got this," Cemil said, patting Rekkus on the shoulder. "She can't be as bad as Sarka."

"I could debate you there," Dana said, but her voice lacked conviction. "Let's get you into your room. There are some rules you need to familiarize yourself with but I'm sure...." Dana sucked in a breath, her hands reached for support. Both men were quick to assist. Although Dana reached for Rekkus, she squeezed Cyrus' gloved hand until her knuckles turned white. Her husband lifted her chin, forcing his wife to focus on him.

Concern etched every inch of his stern face. Rekkus asked in a voice far softer than she thought possible of this man, "What is it, what's wrong?"

"Your son kicked me hard." Dana's voice held even, but Ashlynn could hear the struggle underneath.

"When are the babies due?" her father asked. "I assume there's more than one."

"How did he know? How do you know?" Cyrus threw up his arms in frustration. "Am I the only one not to know?"

Dr. Stone patted his shoulder and chuckled. "I'm an OB/GYN. Years of working with pregnant women gives you a good inkling of such things."

"Dana?" Ashlynn watched her sister force a smile then let out a cry of pain as her lips began to tremble.

"That's it. I am taking you back to our cabin to

rest." Rekkus lifted his wife into his arms as if she was a child instead of a size-eighteen-on-her-skinny-days, pregnant with two babies woman.

"Do I have a say?" Dana laid her head on his shoulder.

Rekkus stopped for a moment and nodded. "The Haus or our home."

"I can walk, Rekkus," she mumbled but, as she closed her eyes, it became obvious she wouldn't make it far. Perhaps the burden of carrying multiples so close to term or maybe the emotional strain of her family dropping by had become too much to bear.

"I'm well aware you can walk, but why do so when I can carry our whole streak. Let me do this for you." Rekkus left the group without so much as a "by your leave."

"He's very protective of her, isn't he?" Ashlynn watched him carry her into the resort. Rekkus had wanted to leave earlier. Although he never pushed, he had made his feelings known. She put her concerns to the back of her mind. He took care of his pregnant wife when Dana had shown signs of not being able to move another step. So why did his manner of control concern Ashlynn?

"You have no idea," Cyrus said with a chuckle. "We here on the island, those who know him best, are still getting used to the softer side of Rekkus."

"Softer?" This was soft? Other than the care he took when he cradled Dana in his arms, Ashlynn had not witnessed a degree of softness in her brother-in-law. Even then she'd seen overprotectiveness, not softness.

"Yeah, softer. Come along. Let's get you settled in." Cyrus waved her toward the Haus.

Tinges of pain edged her brain. Rubbing her

temples, she prayed they could get to her room in time. Where had she packed her meds? "I think I need to lie down. I am not feeling so well."

As they entered the lobby, Cyrus pointed to the line at check-in and winked. "Stay here. I'll be right back."

She didn't have the energy to argue. Cyrus walked behind the receptionist desk, said something to the woman there, and grabbed a key. Placing his hand on the small of her back, he led her to the elevators. "Remember, you must use elevator three. The others won't work for you, or at least they won't go to your floor."

Inside the empty elevator, he pressed the single button. As they rode up, he went through some of the other rules, like never miss dinner. Partway down the hallway to her room, he stopped and cupped her chin. "Trust us and we'll do our best to manage your pain but, without trust, we can do nothing."

"I'll try." Reaching the last room of the hall, he slid the key into the lock, opening the door wide.

"This was your sister's room. It helped in her healing, and I hope it will yours. Get comfortable. I'll find my sister Sage. I think you need her more than any of her other guests do."

"No need." A soft melodic voice filled the room. Around the corner came a small blonde woman, a light to Cyrus' dark. She bore a great resemblance to Cemil. But the eyes would have told her they were siblings. "Cyrus, can you help me pull those curtains? We've had light-reducing drapes added to your windows, Ashlynn, to keep the room dark as you might like it."

Sage moved through the room, plunging it into

forgiving darkness. She appeared to float. Her steps as light as a butterflies wings, she made no sounds, one with her environment. "I'm Sage, but I think you figured that out already. It is such a pleasure to meet Dana's sister."

Ashlynn forced herself not to cringe. She sensed no hostility from the other woman. "I can't imagine she said many good things about me."

"Dana has never spoken a word about you, except to say you existed." Sage approached. "Now, let me examine you."

A wave of pain not associated with her head washed over her. It would have hurt less to have her sister bitch about her than to be thrown into the category of "she lives, but I have nothing else to say about her."

"Do you need more light?"

"No, this is fine. May I touch you?"

Ashlynn nodded, and even the small movement sent shards of agony rippling up her spine. The trigger signs of a killer migraine sent her into a state of nervousness. She had no idea where her meds were and her bags hadn't arrived in her room yet. Stay on top of the pain, her nurse had advised. The darkness of the room helped by easing the sharp stabbing behind her eyes and sudden exhaustion filled her. "May I lie down first?"

"Of course you may."

She braced herself for the prodding and the poking she associated with doctors and nurses. Pleasant surprise filled her at the light brush of fingertips. There was no pain, well, no extra pain. She closed her eyes and allowed Sage to knead her way over her scalp.

"You've been using some of my cream."

"Jessie brought me some in the hospital. I hope you don't mind."

"Don't be silly, I'm happy for you to use it. I'll make some more for you and remind me to make some for Jessie as well. There is little more I can do for your scars, you understand. I'll focus on these headaches. You have one forming, don't you?"

"Can I be of assistance?" Cemil's voice filled the room. Ashlynn hadn't been aware he even entered.

"Perfect timing." Sage patted the bed. "Cemil is going to hold your hand. I want you to relax." Sage's fingers moved from her neck up and over her head. She heard Cemil grunt in conjunction with the tender spots Sage touched. Odd. Only once did the pain get so bad Ashlynn gasped.

"I'm so sorry I had to touch you to assess the damage." More to herself than to Ashlynn, Sage spoke a series of mental notes. "I think we need some butterbur, perhaps willow mixed with a touch of valerian. Yes, that might do it." She returned her attention to Ashlynn. "Your shakes will have peppermint with a good dose of caffeine. I have some candles I think will do the trick, for now, but I have to work up some different soaps and sachets. Okay, to bed you go. I want you to drink the shake I'm leaving you. Take your medicine. It's policy to remove all medications from our guests, but, until I have the right mixture of herbs, I don't want to eliminate your pain relief. I promise the shake tastes better than it looks."

"I can't find my pills," Ashlynn murmured eyes closed, rubbing the bridge of her nose. No sooner were the words out of her mouth than two pills were dropped into her other palm. "Where?"

"Your nightstand," Sage whispered, indicting the orange containers sitting in plain sight.

Ashlynn's stomach protested the thick, ash-colored substance. Then she heard Cyrus' voice whisper trust. So she took a deep breath and gulped. Surprisingly, the shake tasted rather sweet and smooth. She finished it and allowed the two siblings to help tuck her into bed. Her lids grew heavy. Maybe she could rest for a few minutes.

Chapter Three

Shadedor, or Shade as his friends called him, hated these damned portals. He loathed the way they made his insides churn like they were being pulled through his nose. The feeling of having no control and flying though an immense space, the claustrophobia. Each person dealt with them in their own way, and the few times he had talked with others about what they experienced going through them indicated each species had its own issues. Shifters who weren't as powerful could be forced to shift and arrive a tangled mess of animal in human clothing; witches had been known to lose all short-term memory for sometimes days, and his people experienced a sensation of having their souls ripped from them. But portals were a necessary evil and the one way onto the island, at least for him. Due to his paranormal status, he could not ride the ferry without special permission from the Rowan siblings themselves, and, according to the council, he didn't have time to go another route.

Taking a step from the abyss, he walked into the light of the Wiccan Haus. He was somewhat surprised not to find Rekkus guarding the portal. The anonymous security guard greeted him without checking his reservation. Something to broach with Rekkus once they had a moment to chat. Security had been beefed up since a recent breach. All portals to the island had been permanently closed except for the one from Lochmage, the capital city. Even then, those scheduled to travel at unusual times received special charms. Without them, a being would be lost in the abyss until the portal opened back up at sunrise or sunset the next day.

The Syndicate had a handful of charms in their possession for occasions like he found himself in now. The three council members were concerned about the pending labor of Rekkus' mate. With his being the last of his streak and the uncrowned prime of his people, a great deal rode on the babies Dana now carried.

Something big must have happened for Rekkus to be absent from the portal on arrival night. He was not known for delegating where the safety of the Rowans was concerned.

Myron, his favorite gypsy card reader, sat at the reception desk throwing down cards while directing the paranormal group before her to their accommodations. Her hand stopped mid throw as their gaze met.

Violet eyes widened then filled with joy. "Now, you I wasn't expecting. Get over here."

He walked around the long reception desk and into her open arms for a warm hug of welcome. "A kind soul as always." She pulled back as he chuckled. "So you are 'Delphina' now?"

"What? It's the first badge I picked up this morning. So, tell me, what is a soulpath, who doesn't have a reservation, doing here?"

Shade retrieved a letter from the outside pocket of the linen duster he wore and handed it to Myron. It stated by order of the Syndicate he would be allowed on the island for however long as deemed necessary. He'd be given free rein and any other information and all of the assistance he could possibly need...blah, blah, blah.

"Huh?" Myron said, picking up her cards.

He placed his hand on hers, stilling her movement. "No need for you to consult your cards, my friend. It's no secret. I'm here to read Dana and Rekkus' cubs to make sure they are safe and sound. We need to ensure Dana's safety through the last few weeks or days of her pregnancy."

"They send the soul reader?"

"Of course they did," Cemil said in a voice full of goodness and cheer. "Shade, what a wonderful and welcome surprise. I think even Rekkus might relax once he sees you. Well, as much as the man knows how to."

"That is unlikely."

Cemil frowned. He could read anybody's feelings, even if they didn't want him to. One of the most powerful empaths the Syndicate had on record, his powers were at present unrivaled. But Shade had long passed the age where he felt anything. Occasional joy at seeing an old friend, genuine happiness when a new baby came into the world, but true feelings and deep emotions eluded him. He did his job, read his books, and continued living as his people had all done through the centuries. "If you have information you think might upset the tiger, I'm not sure this is the week to share it with him."

"And certainly not the day," Myron said with a nod to Sarka's closed office door.

Interest piqued, he thought to ask more but he would find out the rest later. "I'm here to read the souls. If, as we suspect, one's an alpha male, there is concern with the full moon approaching."

"Sage has the same concern. Rekkus and Cyrus are working with the teen shifters who arrived moments before you did. They are setting them up in the barracks. I can walk you down there. But it's bound to be chaos. We have two alphas these two weeks. One wolf and one bear."

"What kind of bear?"

"Polar."

"Double the trouble."

"Perhaps we should get you set up in a room first." Myron cleared her desk.

"May I request something away from the Haus? Cleanse my paths without the overwhelming sadness I sense here getting in the way. I also sense something else—something sinister."

"Mrs. Stone." Cemil cringed as he rolled his eyes. Even the most patient of men had their breaking point. "Myron, is the cottage on the west coast open?"

"Would you prefer the one on the cliff or on the water?" Myron asked.

"Is there a great deal of active sea life in the area?" He doubted he needed to go into more detail about whether he meant real sea life or were sea life.

"Only Serena, our resident mermaid. But as her husband is here to assist Cyrus and Rekkus during the full moon, she tends to remain close to her harbor except to do her regular checks. Their cottage is next to Rekkus's, so when you see her, explain your needs. She will keep a wide berth and tell others to do the same."

Cemil led Shade to one of the four golf carts used by guests who stayed farther than walking distance from the Haus.

"You've done great things since my last visit."

"What can I say? Helping others is food for the soul."

"Yours seems to be at peace. I hope to meet up with Cyrus. Perhaps I can ease his a little, too."

Cemil's open demeanor closed. "I sense he is pulling away from us at times, but then he is hurt when he is excluded, like today. He has become far better at masking his emotions, making it harder for me to read him. I think he is healing, but I worry he will never be whole."

"Time will tell. If I can help you in any way this week, use me. I sense some tough souls in the Haus." He sensed something strange, not bad or good but new. He couldn't remember the last time anything new came his way.

"You being here is enough. I wish we could send all of our guests packing until after the full moon or, better yet, after the cubs come, but Dana said it would be silly. Perhaps she is right." He shrugged.

"Doesn't take an empath or soulpath to see the whole island is bristling with both excitement and a good dose of concern."

Cemil chuckled then fell silent again for a few moments before saying, "Rekkus' emotions are all over the spectrum and they are strong. His usual ability to keep his emotions in check is absent. I am ill equipped to guard myself against his feelings of anger and concern. Can be somewhat draining."

"It is understandable he can't control them at

present, but it is also understandable you are fighting the surge of such powerful emotions." Shade should have come sooner to assist his friend.

"If it was Rekkus alone it would be hard enough, but then there's Dana and her hormones as well. Have you ever dealt with a pregnant woman's hormones? You would think Dana's were affecting everyone." He rubbed the back of his neck. "Perhaps they are."

"It sounds like you might need to move out of the Haus. Your soul could use a cleanse, my friend." Shade was reading Cemil's soul, and it was concerned.

"You would think it would be easy for me to stay away a night or two, but I can't. We have some unexpected and somewhat-unwelcome guests. I have dealt with worse and survived." Cemil gave a weak smile as he rubbed at his neck.

"Let me cleanse my soul tonight then tomorrow you take this cottage and cleanse yours. We can switch back and forth. There is only so much soul-searching I can do with the twins not yet born, no matter how old their souls might be."

"They sent you out here to read the twins?" Cemil's skepticism washed over Shade.

"They did. Did you think they would send me for another reason?" Shade's presence would be questioned. The lack of trust between the Rowans and the Syndicate had become legendary. Each a necessary evil to the other. But he had remained as neutral to their conflict as one could and still be involved.

"With the Syndicate, one can never be so sure," Cemil said. "Anything you can share about the twins?"

Shade carried packets of information about his objective, information compiled by the best Syndicate seers and psychics. "Nothing yet." He indicated the locked worn-leather satchel. "Not because I won't share, but I don't open the files I am given until I've met my mark. I don't want others' impressions influencing my first reading. I'll read my reports once I've met with Dana. This way I can compare the preciseness of what they collect against mine. Perhaps after dinner I'll stroll down to meet the mama to be. I assume the rules still apply about dinner?"

Cemil nodded. "Don't make Rekkus track you down for dinner. I admit Sage, Myron, and I get a chuckle at how worked up Cyrus and our tiger get over missing guests. Rekkus and his tight-assed rules. Don't tell them, but sometimes we delay a guest on purpose. "

"You have a demented sense of humor, my friend, a trait I've always liked very much."

"Here we are." Cemil parked the cart and threw the keys to Shade. "There's an extra key under the front seat in case you drop this one in the water."

Cemil grabbed the bigger of the two bags and led Shade to an A-frame cottage on a wooden dock above the water. Two sides opened up over the ocean to the fog wall on the horizon. The other two walls offered privacy toward the land with a simple window looking out over the dock. The kitchenette's small stove and refrigerator took up one corner, the rest of the room filled by its round bed, a lounge chair, small table, and a few lamps. A window in the center of the floor offered a view into the ocean below.

Cemil handed him a remote control. "The top

button lowers the walls, the bottom closes the curtains. The window in the floor opens. If you wish to dangle your feet in the water, you'll find the remote control next to the chair, though the water's too cold in my opinion. It's deeper than it appears, so no swimming through it. We've stocked the fridge. You're on a generator, so there are lanterns, candles, and extra blankets in the closets. Bathroom is next to the closet. No luxuries, but the place is quite secluded and, more important, quiet."

"It's perfect." Shade closed his eyes and pushed out over the water. He sensed nothing except for his friend. "Did you turn off the fish?"

"If you sense nothing, Myron must have called in Serena to clear the area. She could easily have circled the island before we got out of view of the house. She is your best defense, so, if you have any problems, jump in the water and yell."

"I can't imagine why I might need help from a mermaid, but thank you."

"I'll leave you in peace. Dinner is in an hour, and perhaps we can discuss a class or two for you to take on while you're here. The deep-meditation class on soul-searching might offer what a few of our guests need."

"Providing you don't ask me to go soul-searching Sarka, I'm your man."

Cemil chuckled as he headed down the pier. Shade waited until he felt the pull and slight pop as the last soul left the area. Rotating his head, he took a deep breath. He couldn't remember the last time he'd experienced silence. Pulling a mat from his backpack, he laid it out and knelt, facing the ocean. For him, silence wasn't only lack of sound. His ability to reach souls was a blessed one, most of the time, but he needed to turn it all off once in a while. He needed peace to replenish his own soul.

He wouldn't complain about his abilities. Others had far worse gifts. Cemil could feel humans' pain miles away, powers even reaching over phone lines. Not a power he wished to possess.

Then there was Cyrus Rowan. No one's gift seemed more of a curse. Other retro-cogs could see the past while the items remained within their touch. Once they let go, the images disappeared as fog does when summer sun reaches high into the sky. Only one born every millennial shared Cyrus' gift. When he touched an item, he could see its history back to its creation, and when he let go, the images remained in his mind. If he touched an assassin's sword, every event the blade had ever been involved in stayed with him, haunted him. He'd once compared the experience to little movies running constantly within his head, ones without an off button.

When everything went bad for Cyrus, it had gone seriously bad. After the assassin who killed his sisters turned his attention to him, he broke. The Syndicate called Shade in to assess the state of Cyrus' soul. It had taken no more than a couple minutes in Cyrus' company for him to make his diagnosis. Walking into the council's high-ceilinged chamber room, Shade informed the three women their vessel could no longer be used.

"Is he fixable?" The elf high priestess whispered.

"Doubtful."

"That bad." The shifting high priestess, voice filled with concern.

"Worse. I think, if he suffers one more trauma,

his soul will shatter."

Silence. Shade sensed they waited for more information, but when dealing with the three, one gave the information they requested, nothing more.

The elf spoke again. "What is your assessment of what would happen then?"

"He would die or he would turn."

"We cannot afford to have our secrets out to our enemies," the vampire queen and oldest council member said in her gravelly voice.

"He is our responsibility. We take care of our own," the elf asserted.

The shifter, most empathic of the trio, asked in a soft voice, "What do you feel he needs?"

"Seclusion, rest, and most of all security. He cannot heal if he doesn't feel he and his family are safe."

"There is an island, small at the moment, but with the ability to grow to adjust to the needs of its owners. The land has been unused for some time, but there is a good-sized German château left by its prior occupants. Might suit his needs," the vampire said.

"It's extremely hard to get to and would provide rest and seclusion," the elf concurred.

Nails tapping their marble desk echoed through the domed room before the shifter spoke. "Security we can supply, but it's the sense of security he needs. It is not something easy to come by—"

"He needs to feel his loved ones are safe. I can think of only one who can give the Rowans everything they need. One who Cyrus trusts above all others," Shade said.

"Rekkus," the three chorused.

"I believe so."

"And how do you propose we get the black-tiger

prince to agree? He is uncompromising on his best days and not a fan of this council," the elf said.

Shade's tension eased as his plan fell neatly into place. "I propose we leave it to Cyrus himself. If we let Rekkus believe this was not a Syndicate decision, he will bend to the needs of his friend."

"Having Rekkus away on an island will prevent an uprising by his hands." The vampiress's tone held a great deal of satisfaction. The Syndicate would relieve themselves of the Rowans while seeming to take care of their own. But it wouldn't be that easy.

Taking a deep cleansing breath, Shade glanced at his watch. His meditation had lasted longer than he'd thought. Standing, he stretched and pulled a sweater out of a suitcase before heading out onto the deck and up the road to the Wiccan Haus for dinner. Living in the Syndicate's capital city of Lochmage, he had little time to take in the joys of nature. Perhaps he could use this week to refresh and rejuvenate his soul. And yet, a tingle nudged at him. The island working its magic, he suspected. The island had grown since his last visit. It appeared to feed off the powers of the Rowans. Were they in turn recharging from its powers? He picked up his pace, propelled toward the Haus and its inhabitants.

Chapter Four

E very bite of food proved better than the last. The chef needed a gigantic raise, even if, for some strange reason, they refused to serve chicken of any kind. Ashlynn savored the flavors, loving the way the tastes exploded in her mouth. She even allowed herself a second plate, enjoying the perks of no longer being a fashion model. But if her mother made one more nasty comment about the Wiccan Haus, Dana, or her second serving, she would pour the food, no matter how scrumptious, over her mother's perfectly coifed head. So far, the staff had gone out of their way to be kind and professional. Their hospitality far exceeded any five-star hotel she'd stayed in. And her mother rewarded their efforts with rude comments and plates being sent back without having been tasted.

Her father sat lost in thought. Perhaps he worried for Dana. His daughter being heavily pregnant with twins and far from modern conveniences of the city or one of his hospitals must weigh heavy on his mind. The echo of her sister's name being repeated throughout the dining room preceded her arrival. As Dana's husband guided her across the room, a gentle hush fell. Many staff members approached them, rubbing the pregnant belly with affection. Envy overcame Ashlynn. All of the island residents would come to visit her sister in her confinement, help without being asked. They loved her, and she smiled at them, returning their love. Only three people had come to see Ashlynn in the hospital, not including her parents. Her agent, her lawyer, and Dana's best friend.

What did that say about Ashlynn? She spent too many hours traveling on photo shoots, had been tutored rather than attending school so she had never made a true friend growing up, and the one thing she had come to rely on, long hours on runways and photo shoots, had been taken from her. But if her sister could start again and find so much happiness, Ashlynn could, too.

Dana cast Rekkus a pleading look, and finally Rekkus inclined his head. Dana sat at the table with her family; Rekkus stood at her shoulder as if waiting to pounce. Her mother parted her lips to speak then snapped them closed under his glare. To watch Rekkus tear into her mother would be a treat. Dana greeted their father with a kiss on the cheek, but their mother ignored her presence. Ashlynn tried to make amends until a stilling hand told her Dana didn't need them. "How is your head? I heard you had a rough afternoon."

She guessed privacy acts didn't stretch to the resort, not that she cared if her sister knew she had a headache. But after weeks in the hospital where no one could tell anyone she had asked for an aspirin, it was a change to have her business known. "Surprisingly okay, now. I guess I needed a nap."

"I can relate. All I do is nap these days." Dana glanced up at her husband. "Honey, if you need to be somewhere else, I'll be fine."

His attention moved to Dana then to his mother-in-law and back to his wife. "I can see everyone I need to from here, and there is no way I am leaving your side."

"Are you saying for once everyone showed up for dinner?"

Cyrus, who had been circling the dining room, joined them. "Oh, three didn't show up but your mate—husband sent Kaleb after them."

"Rekkus!"

A boyish smile softened the big man. "What? It was Cyrus' idea."

"Might have been." Cyrus shrugged. "Serves him right. We did have to get his ass here a number of times while he was a guest. Payback's a bitch."

Ashlynn marveled at how Dana brought two men to heel, changing them from monstrous walls of fearsomeness to most youthful in their behavior. Like two children with their hands caught in the cookie jar, each claiming the other started it. "I'm impressed."

Dana's brow creased. "At what?"

"When you say jump, do they also ask how high?"

She smiled, "Ah. Neither is tamed, but they occasionally let me believe I'm in control."

"You might want to inform your sister I have excellent hearing." Rekkus leaned between the two of them. "What do you want for dinner, Dana? The kitchen is unsure what to send out."

"Can you ask Cherry for a steak—rare? Some Roosevelt beans and corn on the cob with extra butter."

"And?"

"And maybe some corn bread."

"Do they serve to order here? I asked for chicken and they said no...." Green colored her sister's face and her hands shot to her mouth. "Dana?"

"Whatever you do, don't mention poultry. Makes her a bit sick to her stomach," Cyrus whispered in her ear.

"Can't have it in the building. She can smell it a mile away—raw or cooked, doesn't matter," Rekkus said.

Cyrus straightened. "I'll put her order in."

"Rekkus, could you either sit down or do something? You're making me nervous." Ashlynn shifted uncomfortably.

"It's what he does best." A man in the uniform of a security guard paused at her side. Despite his significant height, he stood shorter than the rest of the guards. He seemed different somehow, more down to earth. No less buff but more approachable. "Last guest is accounted for."

This must be Kaleb. Rekkus nodded.

"The last guest isn't on the roster, Rekkus. And he would like to talk to you and Cyrus as soon as possible."

Rekkus rounded on the shorter man. "What do you mean not on the roster?"

Kaleb stood his ground. "He had a letter granting him permission to come on-site this week."

"Fucking Syndicate and their damned minions. And why am I only now being informed of his arrival?" Happy his gruff tone was directed elsewhere, Ashlynn focused on her food.

"Rekkus, brusque as always. Some things never change." Ashlynn turned toward the door at the voice warm and smooth enough to melt butter.

"What the hell are you doing here?" Rekkus growled but, to Ashlynn's surprise, smiled.

Gorgeous did not describe this man. There was something absolutely...absolute about him. His piercing green eyes sparked like emeralds. His long dark hair, the color of midnight on a moonless night, lay like silk against his broad shoulders. And although not as tall as Rekkus and Cyrus, he made her six-foot figure seem petite.

"Close your mouth, sis. You're gonna catch flies."

"Are all the men on this island related to Adonis?" Statistically, the amount of gorgeousness in this room didn't make sense.

Dana leaned into her and giggled. "Some might say so."

"Don't you think having one daughter marry beneath her is enough for this family without your drooling over the help?" Venom dripped from her mother's lips, and conversation around the table ceased. How could she have even for a moment forgotten her presence?

"She speaks," Dana said into the stillness.

Nancy Stone's nose rose another inch into the air. "When it's something of utmost importance."

"Don't you mean when something might result in the happiness of Ashlynn that doesn't involve you?"

Ashlynn gaped. Dana had never before shown a backbone. She had respected and obeyed every command as if she were Cinderella.

"Why you ungrateful—"

"Nancy, enough." Their father lifted his focus from his food as if coming out of a trance.

"It is not enough. Our daughter needs plastic surgery in a hospital. Not this new-agey place. And she's gained twenty pounds in the last month." Her mother's disgust made Ashlynn feel three years old again.

"My modeling career is over. It doesn't matter how many plastic surgeons I see. My face will forever be damaged goods." She pointed to the long scar under her ear. "Nothing is going to change."

"Being here on this island, with her"—their mother turned her gaze on Dana for the first time— "and all of these hippies will not help you. She is the size of a small bear."

Everything happened so quickly, Ashlynn couldn't process it all. One second Rekkus was staring down his mother-in-law, the next he was on the other side of the table, his face only inches from hers. Ashlynn could have sworn he jumped over the table, and where had the growl come from?

But beyond the chaos, a sudden cold chill ran through her, as if someone had opened a door to the arctic. She could see her breath. She couldn't see Rekkus' face, but the fear covering her mother's made an impression. She had never seen her mother cower. She had never seen anger like she did in her brother-in-law.

Sage and Cemil appeared from out of nowhere, and Cyrus ran from the other side of the room. As if sensing it wouldn't do any good, no one touched or grabbed Rekkus.

Sage's soft voice broke through the tension. "Perhaps Mrs. Stone would like to return to her room for the evening."

"I would not."

"I could drop you into a cavernous hole if you would prefer," Rekkus said.

Sage moved a little closer to him, her calm extending over the table. "Let me restate the rules of the Haus. If you cannot be polite to others, we cannot have you in the dining room or in classes with other people. This is a place of healing. I will not have you disrupt the healing of others out of pettiness on your account."

Their mother's eyes blazed. "He attacked me, and I am being reprimanded?"

Cemil placed a hand on her elbow and guided her to her feet. "Had he attacked you, there would be very little any of us could do to stop it and even less of you left to identify."

"They're right, Nancy. You are disruptive and acting like a spoiled child." Dr. Stone's gaze landed on Myron, who joined the others around the table. "Is your offer for a separate room still available?"

Myron dangled a key before him. How had she known of the request before he made it? "The room is ready."

"Rekkus," Tall, Dark, and Awesome said in a low tone. "Her soul is dark. Do not let hers affect yours."

Rekkus gave a jerk of his chin which passed as a nod. "Stay out of my sight," he tossed over his shoulder as he stormed out of the dining hall.

"That man is an animal!" Nancy announced.

Dana got to her feet and, for the first time in Ashlynn's experience, stood up for herself. "You have no idea, Mother, and I pray you never do. This is my home, and I will not have you making our lives hell. Just because you're miserable does not give you the right to make everyone else unhappy, too. If you think for one second I give a damn what you think of me anymore, you can think again. The time of you being able to bully me around, belittle me, or make me feel less of a person is over."

"You will not talk to me in that tone of voice, young lady."

"Oh, shut up. You might think you hold clout in New York City, but here you are a guest like everyone else. But, unlike everyone else, no one wants to be with you. So here are your choices. You can continue to be ill-mannered and insulting to everyone, in which case I will give my husband full permission to lock you in the kennel like the bitch you are, or you can show some breeding and class and start to act like a human being for once."

The room became icy and quiet, everyone's attention locked to her sister, and Ashlynn couldn't have been prouder. Perhaps the hormones raging through her system or a backbone she grew while here on the island accounted for her candor, but it had been too long in coming and Dana had reached her breaking point.

"Dana, have some chocolate cake. You earned it," the man across the table said with a smile, pushing the cake toward her. "I realize your dinner hasn't arrived, but sometimes dessert first is a win-win for everyone."

Dana's face lit up, but a sheen of tears edged her walnut-colored eyes. She took her seat and focused her energy on the dessert before her.

Ashlynn turned to the man and whispered, "Thank you for defusing the situation."

"Is that what I did?" he said, taking a bit of cake from another plate. Had he had two? "I thought I announced the arrival of dessert. Here, try some."

Without hesitation, she allowed this stranger to feed her from his fork. Wrapping her lips around the tines, she savored the moist chocolate piece of heaven he gave her. "Oh my."

"The kitchen staff is some of the best there is and they have, from what I am told, been enjoying catering to the needs of the mama to be over there, because usually such things as chocolate cake aren't on the menu."

"That is a crime." She could listen to his voice all night long. It soothed her. The more he spoke, the calmer she felt.

"I must agree." His green eyes sparked with merriment as he took another bite. When he finished his cake, he left his fork on the empty plate. "Pardon me for saying this, Ashlynn, but I don't believe there is a thing this place can do to help you or your mother."

"No pardon needed. She has never been mother of the year and isn't going to open herself up to alternative practices anytime soon."

He reached across the table in greeting. "We haven't been properly introduced. I am Shadedor, but my friends simply call me Shade."

"A pleasure—Ashlynn Stone." As her fingers touched his, a tingle ran all the way up her arm. Heat pooled in her belly, and her mouth went dry. New sensations blending with the sudden rise in temperature in the room made her light-headed. Taking off her sweater, she eyed her sister engaged in happy conversation with Cyrus. "What is it with the temperature changes in this place?"

Shade squinted at Dana before returning his attention to Ashlynn. "They must have turned up the heat. The island can get chilly at night. Have we met before?"

"Is that a pickup line?"

"No, but if it worked, then we can use it."

"Um, not so much."

He laughed, the sound rusty as if he didn't do it much, and laid his napkin on his empty plate. "I have seen you somewhere before."

And here it came. Discover she had been a famous model and he would be curious about her superficial life, a life she wanted to forget. "I have one of those faces, I guess."

"No, it's something else.... You are on the billboard outside my flat in London. The face of some makeup company or was it beer?"

"I was the face." She ran her fingers down the scar, remembering the moment when the light hit her.

He reached out to grab her hand. "Don't hide who you are. You are beautiful, scars and all. The scars might make you imperfect, but they also make you interesting. You have a story. It makes you unique."

How did a man she just met know the exact words her soul craved to hear?

"Shade with all the commotion, I didn't get to welcome you, my friend." Cyrus came around the table and embraced Shade as he stood. "Do you ever age?"

"Yes, but extremely slowly. How are you?"

He shrugged. "Eh—it's a process I suppose."

"Still healing?"

"It is a journey we all take in our own time." Cyrus lowered his voice. "I want to get Dana home, so perhaps tomorrow we can catch up."

"Tomorrow is perfect. I need to meet with Dana and Rekkus, but tonight I feel is not the night. Perhaps in the morning."

The mention of her sister had Ashlynn turning in her direction. Her sister's pale cheeks and drooping eyelids sent a pang of worry through her. Although she had eaten the first few bites of her chocolate cake with enthusiasm, she pushed the remaining part around her plate. Ashlynn wanted to cheer her for telling her mother off, to plead with her not to let the old hag affect her, but who was she to talk? Their mother had her master's degree in finding the right barbs to throw and knowing where to aim them. No doubt she worked up a string of them now.

"Ashlynn," Cyrus said, a friendly smile curving his lips, "I believe you have a busy evening of relaxation ahead of you. First reflexology and then deep breathing with Trixie."

"Dana didn't eat, even the cake." She twisted her napkin, worry for her sister seeping out. "She only took a few bites."

"Ash, I'm fine. Exhausted but okay."

"You have nothing to worry about. The staff always ensures your sister has what she needs. Most of the time before she asks for it. She is, after all, our family." Cyrus helped Dana to her feet and wrapped a brotherly arm around her. Smiling at Ashlynn again, he led Dana from the room.

"Your sister will be fine. It's been a hard day for everyone. And one Rekkus and, I think, many on the island have been dreading," Shade assured her as the pair escaped from view.

"What do you mean?"

"Rekkus has done his best to keep your family away."

"He has that." Ashlynn wondered now if Dana's lack of communication with anyone in the family had been at Rekkus' insistence. After all, with one phone and one computer conveniently guarded behind the front desk, how hard would it be for him to prevent her from contacting anyone? Jessie came back to visit, but hadn't she said the last visit had been at Rekkus' request?

"Rekkus can act overbearing at times but remember when she arrived here, raw, hurting, and depressed at your mother's rejection? The woman Rekkus met had been broken down."

It made sense. "How would you know any of this?"

"Their souls speak to me."

Cemil started coughing so loud one of the wait staff brought him a glass of water.

"Their souls as in the force within them?" Ashlynn inched away a bit in her chair. What kind of healing could this man be here for anyway?

"Yes, you see—"

"Right...okay. I think I am going to head on to my reflexology appointment." Throwing her white napkin down in surrender, Ashlynn pushed back from the table.

"Can I escort you to your destination?"

"No thanks." Before Shade could stand, she worked her way through the maze of tables and out the door. She stayed focused on the hallway before her. Bummer Tall, Dark, and Handsome was quite whacko. Just her luck.

"What just happened?" Shade asked no one in

particular. Her soul, open and receptive, had, in a matter of seconds, slammed shut to him.

"It could be because she has no knowledge about anything to do with the para world," Cemil said, shaking his head. "If you had acknowledged me when I began my coughing fit, you might have saved face. I wasn't at all subtle in trying to get your attention."

"How can she still be in the dark? Her brother-in-law is a tiger shifter."

"Until today, Dana hasn't spoken to any of her family since she left the mainland. No one took her calls or received her letters. Her mother, as you have discovered, is a force unto herself, and effectively disowned her."

"So they have no idea Dana, when she gives birth to the cubs, will take on the title of queen?"

Cemil sighed. "I don't honestly know if Dana is aware of the title, but I don't think even knowing he is royalty would help the situation. I'm somewhat surprised you couldn't assess all this on your own."

"Her soul, though interesting, isn't what caught my attention."

"After one hundred and fifty years, your libido has reawakened?"

"You make it sound like I never get laid."

Cemil arched a brow. Who did Shade think he fooled? "When did you last get laid?"

"Seventy-five years, give or take a year." When a person didn't feel much, sex for the sake of pleasure got old quickly. He had lost interest sometime after the Great War.

Cemil choked. "I have no words."

"And you? When was the last time you got laid?"

"We aren't talking about me, and the pool for me to choose from is much smaller than yours, oh world traveler."

"Until this evening, I had no interest. But, with my kind, that is the way it happens." They would go decades, sometimes centuries, until they found someone who started a spark. For many, the spark would fade following intercourse or at the next full moon. His father, a shaman, had stayed long enough to learn about his mother's pregnancy. The spark had faded with the cresting of the full moon weeks before. It had been better, in a way. She would be taken care of and, unlike humans of the time period, she wouldn't be shunned but revered for her fertility.

He met his father sometime after his thirtieth year, an amicable and informative encounter, but Shade felt no desire to see the man again. They had connected several times over the last century as his job with the Syndicate had brought him in contact with most talented magicians, his father the top shaman. Later, the same connections would have him crossing paths with the Duteigr Streak, Rekkus' pack, and the Rowans.

Pulling out of his musing, he met Cemil's twinkling eyes. "But it's never happened with one like her."

"I suggest you try and act more like her, then. More human."

Human? How did one act human, and what did a soulpath do when his abilities were clouded by intense sexual desires he hadn't felt in decades, if ever? Their inherent lack of emotion allowed them to deal with souls and be unaffected. An ability Cyrus should have been blessed with.

"You'll figure it out, my friend." Cemil patted him on the shoulder and walked off, leaving Shade to eat

---

the rest of his meal in silence. The others at his table had left to follow their own pursuits.

He scanned the room for no other reason than to get his mind off Ashlynn Stone. In the dark-green section of the dining hall, a few paras still dined, including one with shifting issues—never an easy thing for a shifter to admit—and two witches healing from spells gone wrong. In the light-green section, he observed a young couple with infertility issues and an older couple dealing with Parkinson's, and, in the back, between the two sides, a mermaid in love.

The Siren caught him off guard. Mermaids showed little emotions, and this one radiated both kindness and love. Well, miracles never ceased. So what did one do when he was supposed to act human normal?

A question he had no answer for.

Chapter Five

It didn't matter if he was crazy. She wanted him with a desire she had never experienced in her life. This pull to him unbearable, tied her stomach in knots. Sleep, when it graced her, came in broken naps and fretful bouts. Her traitorous body and erotic dreams kept luring her back to images of his green eyes set against his tanned skin. She needed to focus on healing, on finding a cure for her headaches, and coming to terms with her scars. Scars she discovered cut as deep inside as they did out.

A headache had hit her so hard during her relaxation class she'd curled into a fetal ball. She had no recollection of how she came to be back in her room with an eye mask over her face, lavender filling her senses, and Sage's soothing voice whispering orders to those around her.

A single candle gave the room what little light she needed as Sage chanted something in a language Ashlynn didn't recognize. The sounds and cadence soothed. Twice she awakened to find Sage sitting in the chair beside her, a kind smile always gracing her soft face.

"How did I get back here?" she remembered asking at some point.

"My brother Cyrus brought you here."

"You don't have to stay."

"Of course I do. You need me."

Her own mother couldn't be bothered to sit more than half an hour and this virtual stranger whom her sister called family sat all night in case the headache returned. No wonder Dana never came home. Not with people this welcoming and warm to stay for. Even the imposing Rekkus showed moments of softness her mother could not summon.

"Why are you crying?" Sage asked, concern marring her perfect brow. "Is the pain back?"

Shaking her head, she buried her face in the pillow. How could she overcome such sadness and the realization she had never been given motherly love?

Sage climbed into the bed and embraced Ashlynn, holding her tight and secure as she wept. When the sun came up, she slept, dreaming of a tall, dark man with skin the color of melted caramel, eyes the color of shamrocks in the Irish countryside, and hair of silken black.

She awoke refreshed, filled with a new vigor as if the world might not be a painful thing.

"You're awake." A whisper washed over her and the voice soothed her mind. "Shall I call Sage?"

"No, not yet. Who are you?" The curtains were closed, leaving the room drenched in forgiving darkness. She sat up, hesitant at first, surprised to find the woman at her side to assist.

She passed Ashlynn a glass tumbler. "Sage said you must drink this before you start your day. I'm Serena. Is there anything I can do for you?"

"Are you another Rowan?"

"No, I am a staff member but at one time a guest, too." Serena walked across the room, humming as she picked up a blanket which lay on the floor in a puddle of fabric.

"What's the tune you are humming?"

"I didn't mean to hum. I am so sorry." Horror pinched the woman's beautiful face.

"Please continue. It's...." Searching for the right word, she bit her lip before deciding on, "Comforting."

Serena smiled and hummed as she straightened the room. "Drink up and I'll go draw you a bath."

"What time is it?" The room had no clock. Considering the place ran on tight timetables for classes, Ashlynn had yet to see a clock.

Serena cocked her head to the side and stood stock-still. "Six, I would guess from the tides."

Mid sip, Ashlynn stopped. The tides? Was everyone crazy here? Or perhaps the loony bin had been disguised as a resort. Focusing on her shake, she decided to roll with whatever came at her. After all, what did she have to lose? A slight knock on the door sounded, and Serena opened the door enough for the other woman to chat with whomever came to the door but not enough to allow the person to come in. Although she couldn't tell whom she talked to, Serena apologized in hushed tones for something.

"Take a chill, girl." Cyrus came into the room, removing his dark glasses and resting them on his head. She realized the last couple of times she had seen him he even had worn those glasses even at night. "I'm here at Sage's bequest to check on her patient and see how your head is."

"Much better this morning. I should thank you. Sage informed me you were the one who helped me back here last night."

"It is the least I could do. Luckily, I happened to be close by when Shade rang the alarm."

Crazy, sexy hunkman? "Shade?"

"Yes, he can sense when a soul's in pain."

"Soul?"

"Soul...person. It's very much the same thing really." Cyrus smiled, and she wondered why no modeling agency had ever picked this man up. Granted, all the men here were gorgeous, but something dark and mysterious made him a bit more dangerous. Even beautiful. "It occurred to Shade that part of your issue might be the lights."

"But Trixie had no lights."

"No, but she did say she had the class focus on the flames of a bonfire." Oh, his smile would get anyone to agree. "We have created a special pair of glasses we think could help you."

"Are they like yours?"

"No, why would you ask?"

"Well, you wear them all the time."

Cyrus gave a sad smile. "It's so my family doesn't worry or see my suffering."

Unsure what to say, she nodded. She eyed the gloved hands and wondered what kind of scars forced him to cover up at all times. Had he been burned, deformed, or was he hiding the ugly scars of an accident?

"Some of us wear our scars on the inside. Some lucky people have them on the outside." He brushed over the scar on her face, lingering over the burn on her neck. She should have pulled away but found the soft touch of the glove soothing. His inner strength or power drew her. Not sexually like Shade, but mentally.

"Lucky? I can't think anyone would call me lucky."

He drew back. "Yes, lucky. You show the world your pain, your struggles. Every time you walk outside, you prove to those who hurt you that you survived. You have strength and they can't defeat you."

Grabbing his hand in hers, she asked, "What about the inside scars? What do you do for those?"

"Oh, dear lady, I had hoped you would be able to tell me."

Butterflies much like those that formed when one was about to be kissed for the first time fluttered in the pit of her stomach. It connected them, their understanding of one another. "If I knew, I would tell you."

"I promise the same." He moved back to the front door where he had dropped a bag. Pulling out a hard case, he removed a pair of black-rimmed glasses "They aren't the height of fashion but should do for this week to help you acclimate to the lenses. If they work, we can send the prescription to a special optometrist in New York to get them set into something more stylish."

"At this point, haute couture is the last thing on my mind." She rested the frames on the brim of her nose and, in the darkness of the room, could no longer even make out his silhouette.

"That's the spirit. Ready to give them a try in the light?"

She nodded, closing her eyes as he pulled back the curtains. With a great deal of trepidation, she lifted one lid then the other, allowing her the time needed to adjust to the glasses and the light. The lenses created a silvery effect.

"It will take some getting used to." Cyrus laid steadying hands on her shoulders. "But, for now, tell me what you see or, as it might be, what you cannot."

"I see shapes. Nothing in focus."

"As you train your eyes, they will see what is there and your brain will fill in the rest."

She tensed. Her world would become shades of silver, not even black and white. No color or real images to latch onto. She was, had always been a visual person. Fashion, theater, and art her forms of enjoyment. Now they were stripped from her.

His hands tightened. "This isn't forever, Ashlynn."

"How can you be so sure?"

"I have faith in the powers of my sisters and in their abilities to heal."

"I feel like I have lost my faith." She didn't know where those words came from, but they tore from her. Tears pooled behind her lids, and, before she could turn away, do what she did best, hide her emotions as her mother trained her to do, he supported her in the strength of his arms. Warm and caring, taking on her issues as if they were his own.

"Your pain is tearing me apart," he ground out into her hair. His lips brushed the top of her scalp.

The bathroom door opened, and Serena strolled out. Ashlynn had forgotten the presence of the other woman. Cyrus jumped back a foot. "Your bath is ready as Sage requested. Did I interrupt something?"

Cyrus regained his composure first. "Not at all."

Serena smiled and headed back into the bathroom. "Whenever you are ready."

"She didn't believe that for a second." Ashlynn giggled.

"You might be surprised. She is a bit naive sometimes."

"No one is that naive."

"I wouldn't bet on it." Cyrus said his good-byes to both ladies before taking his leave.

Ashlynn entered the bathroom and waited to be left in private. When it became obvious the blonde intended to stay, Ashlynn sighed, undressed, and climbed into the warm bath. The scented water made her skin tingle and yet it took on the sensation of liquid satin.

Relaxing, she lay back as Serena began to hum. "Do you sing as well?"

"I do but I am not permitted to."

"Not allowed?"

She nodded and shrugged as if it were not surprising. "Rekkus would have my fin if I sang a single note."

"Do you mean hide?"

"Pardon?"

"He will have your hide? But what right does he have to say you can't sing. What kind of control freak is he?"

"He controls almost every aspect of the island, but then, to maintain safety...." She shrugged.

The gnawing feeling rose again. Perhaps her sister didn't have much choice when it came to staying here or not. Ashlynn had tried to push the kernel of concern to the back of her mind, but it kept creeping forward. "Do you know where my sister might be?"

"'This early in the morning? Still in her cabin,

most likely. I can ask Rekkus."

"Does he know her every move on the damned island?" Maybe her words came out nastier than she meant it to, but the other woman seemed oblivious to the venom.

"Pretty much, and more so as Dana gets closer to her time."

Sitting up, Ashlynn wrapped her arms around her bare legs, bringing her knees to her chest. "Can I ask you something?"

"Of course."

"Has Dana ever left the island? I mean, since she arrived here."

"I don't think so. I haven't always been here, but every time I came back after meeting her the first time, she was here. When Sage goes to the mainland, Rekkus gives her a shopping list for Dana."

"Is she happy?" After all, she could be putting on a brave face for her family. It wasn't as if Dana would trust any of them to step in and help. They had already proved lacking in taking care of their own.

"She loves him, if that is what you mean. She does tend to throw things at him when she is angry. My husband and I are their neighbors. Kaleb, my husband, gets a great deal of enjoyment in watching Rekkus deflect her temper."

Ashlynn lay back down and wondered how bad things had to get for her mellow and level-headed sister to throw things at anyone. How controlling was this brother-in-law of hers?

***

Shade knocked on the door of Rekkus' cabin at

eight-thirty sharp. He had been assured Rekkus would be available and Dana ready for his arrival. The two cabins had been placed off the beaten path enough for most guests, para and human alike, to stay away. In case those deterrents weren't enough, the guards who stood watch up the hill would fend off any others. The smells of fresh-cut wood and paint assailed his nostrils, and he saw why. An addition had been made to accommodate the growing family within.

His cleanse hadn't been as pure as he'd hoped for the evening before. His mind kept drifting back to Ashlynn Stone whose scarred beauty haunted him as much as her masked pain. When her soul cried in distress, he heeded the call and ran to her as if his life depended on it. She affected him in a way no other woman had. Her touch electrified him, and he longed to learn what else she could affect.

Rekkus threw open the door, naked as the day he came into the world. Shifters, mermaids, and even some witches seemed oblivious to the fact the majority of people did not walk around naked.

"Let me get dressed. My morning rounds took longer than expected."

"Security in the nude? A new concept even for you."

"I do it as my tiger."

"I was joking."

"So you say," he called from the bedroom.

Dana mumbled something before Rekkus said in a voice far gentler than he had ever heard from the man, "Stay in bed, luv. You were up all night, and no one will think anything of your being lazy for a day. Go back to sleep."

Shade moved closer to the open bedroom door. "May I come in? I can read the cubs as easily with her lying down. She can even sleep through it."

"One second." The gruff protective voice he expected from Rekkus. "Dana, where is that bloody nightgown of yours?"

Only Rekkus could walk around butt naked and still care if Dana lay covered in a sheet. After a bit of rustling and a few more grumbles from both, they bid him to enter. Surveying the sparse room of natural tones and wooden furniture, Shade allowed his gaze to come back to the heavily pregnant woman lying on her side in bed. He needed to assess if anything in the room could interfere with his reading. Family heirlooms might contain traces of ancestors' souls. Especially from Rekkus' family who had all died horrific deaths at the hands of his mother. His focus locked on the lepidolite ring on a chain around Dana's neck.

"Sorry to have woken you, Dana." He kept his voice low and soft.

"I would have been up in a few minutes anyway." She struggled to prop herself up on a few pillows. Rekkus, by her side in an instant, helped lift her and placed two cushions behind her.

"Before we start, can I ask you to remove the ring around your neck?"

She gripped the ring as if protecting it. "My wedding ring?"

"It belonged to my sister, Eiriana. She gave it to me before she died." Rekkus stood, arms crossed beside the bed. "Sarka transmuted it for Dana before we mated."

"If it's Eiriana's, that explains it. Dana, you can have it back once I am done with my reading. But, for now, I need to remove anything that might interfere. I am here to read the cubs and see how they fair."

"Please call them babies." The hitch in her voice as she said those words told him the sensitivity of the topic.

"My apologies. Perhaps Rekkus could take your ring and order you some breakfast while we get started."

"Is that your polite way of saying you would prefer me out of the room?"

It was never easy telling a loved one their absence garnered the best results from their significant other while Shade worked, but convincing a shifter—more to the point, Rekkus—to leave his mate and cubs, his babies, he didn't relish. "Your soul is, how do I put this, stronger than most."

"Not just his soul." Dana removed the necklace and gave it in Rekkus. "Perhaps you should take my grandmother's watch as well."

Rekkus nodded, opening the nightstand drawer to remove an antique watch. The mysterious hum increased. "Yes, very helpful."

"Do you want your usual for breakfast?"

Shaking her head, she licked her lips. "Can I get a rare steak and some milk? Make that a lot of milk."

Rekkus' eyebrows shot up a bit at the request, but he gave a short bow to kiss his wife's forehead before walking out of the room, leaving the door open. There were only so many provisions one could ask of the mated shifter.

"May I?" Shade indicated the space on the bed next to Dana. She nodded and followed it with a yawn. "Having a hard time sleeping?"

"For weeks."

"Sit back and relax. You don't have to do anything." Although she tried to relax, he could sense her soul in conflict with his being here. She didn't understand and was terrified he might find something wrong with her babies. "Because you are the mother, your soul is going to fight against me getting to your...children. If I touch your belly, I will be able to read them better and help put your mind at ease."

She tensed, and, for a minute, nothing could get through her protections. For a human, she was highly in touch with her inner self.

"Tell me about your family. I understand you haven't seen them since you left the mainland."

Dana opened her eyes in shock, as he'd hoped, and he snuck past her defenses. One of the first things his kind learned, the ability to talk to someone, in fact carry on intelligent conversations while letting his soul talk to theirs.

Shade smiled, rubbing her extended abdomen. Closing his eyes, he reached out to the cubs, Dana would deal with terminology later, but, for now, he needed to treat them as young and protective para shifters. He reached out and felt the slight push of curiosity from the first baby. Definite male and strong, he came to the forefront. Shade played it easy, and he spoke to the little one of love and protection. "Easy. I am here to help ensure your mum is safe."

Dana rubbed her belly, still answering questions Shade verbally asked. She didn't like talking about her parents. Particularly her mother, but it kept her mind off the babies for a minute. The second cub, more curious, came forward but didn't block. He pushed back. Shade hadn't expected this. The first, though an alpha, acted as guard to the second, who he read as a prime. For any prime to stand behind another meant he protected something or someone else.

Shade stopped talking and removed his hand from Dana's belly before replacing it higher and to the side. Rekkus must have sensed something because he stood at his full, imposing height in the doorway, concern marring his brow as he laid the food tray on the dresser. "What is it?"

As Rekkus' voice reached the babies, a shift occurred. Not the sudden chill Rekkus' concern brought to the room but through the protection of the two came...another. "Well, well, well aren't you a little surprise."

"Shade, what have you found?" Rekkus growled, and the air temperature dropped until Shade could see his breath.

He beckoned Rekkus over. "Easy, Da. Come rub your mate's belly and tell your sons to stand down."

Rekkus climbed onto the mattress on the other side of Dana, rested his hands on her belly, and spoke. "Hawdd fy meibion, gadewch ein cyfaill i mewn."

The two boys moved to the side as Rekkus continued to chant in Welsh. Easy, my sons, let our friend in. "There you are, my sweet."

"Rekkus?" Dana asked eyes wide with concern.

"Everyone is fine, but you appear to have three babes inside this beautiful round tummy of yours."

"That's not possible. They did an ultrasound." Rekkus' head shot up.

"You would believe a machine over me? Easy, tiger, your daughter has been hiding or has been hidden by her brothers to protect her. Have either of you noticed strange weather events or unexplained temperature changes?"

"This is the Wiccan Haus. Most of what happens here I cannot explain," Dana grumbled, eyeing the plate of food across the room. As if sensing her need, Rekkus rose from the bed and brought the tray forward. Dana, ignoring the fork, picked up the steak and bit into it. "Oh, so good."

Shade shook his head in a silent communication to not say anything. She might be human and a perfect lady, but it took a lot of food and strength to nourish three cubs. After a few bites, she came up for air. "I have noticed a lot more changes in the weather, quicker and more changeable, if that makes sense. Especially when Rekkus is angry or upset."

"Thunder and rain, maybe?"

"I guess, I mean it rained last night," Dana muttered between bites as she tore into the steak like a tiger in the wild tore into its prey.

"Did it? Because it didn't rain at my cabin or at the main Haus."

"Are you saying one of the cubs is an elemental empath?" Rekkus asked.

Dana lifted her face from chugging her milk. "A what?"

Rekkus reached over with a napkin to wipe her away her milk moustache. " Elemental empath or EE. It's a special power. The bearer can affect the weather with their emotions."

"Was one of you upset last night?"

"You would have thought with my family's sudden appearance on the island it would have been me. But I was too exhausted to care by the end."

When Shade moved his attention to Rekkus, the man shrugged. "I might have some pent-up anger directed toward the Stones."

"They aren't all bad, Rek. My father and sister genuinely want to make amends. My mother...." She shrugged but her soul screamed out in pain.

"The bitch is...a bitch."

Thunder rolled outside, and rain hit the window panes. Baby C had attuned itself with Rekkus, which cemented the thoughts forming in his head. "Rekkus, this babe is affected by you. Your sister had the powers of an EE, didn't she?"

"Eiriana was a very powerful EE."

"You were close?" Shade almost doubled over as pain so raw and close to the surface ripped through Rekkus. Taking a deep, cleansing breath, Shade put up a hand. "Easy, I believe your sister has chosen to return to you."

Shade explained in terms Dana could comprehend that some souls returned when their time had been cut too short. But all memories would be wiped away at their first breath. "I think you two have some information to process, and I'll leave you to do so. But should you have any questions—"

The door to the cabin flew open, and a soaking-wet Cyrus strode into the bedroom. The tiger would not let any other man into his mate's bedroom. Cyrus' presence played testament to the pair's relationship. "Do you realize it's raining over your cabin again? What the hell, Rekkus?"

Shade excused himself, leaving it to the couple to share or not as they chose. But he did catch Rekkus saying in a tone befitting a king, "I believe it's time to start the process of shutting the portal down if only temporarily."

A great plan. Rekkus couldn't protect the

Rowans while his mate labored, and her time approached. Word would have circled the gossip mills, and, even with no one knowing the gestational times for mixed breeds, people would guess she was growing close.

Chapter Six

T he deep-tissue massage had been what Ashlynn needed, but within five minutes of sitting at the lunch table with her mother, every one of her muscles locked right back up again.

"Really, Ashlynn, those are the most hideous sunglasses I have ever seen. Do take them off. They are ruining my appetite."

"They help my head," she said, refusing to remove them.

"I don't particularly care, dear. They make you look like a bag lady."

"I think they are rather cute," Shade's deep voice said from behind her. "May I join you?"

"Please." She indicated the empty seat across from them then closed her eyes and allowed the appearance of him last night to fill her senses. When she opened them, she saw a better image of him through the shimmer. Cyrus had been correct. Her brain would fill in the areas her optic nerve missed. "I understand I have you to thank for rescuing me last night."

"Last night?" her mother asked in a tone usually

reserved for Dana alone, leaving Ashlynn to wonder how her sister had dealt with it for all those years.

"Your daughter had an episode last night. I happened to get her help before it got too bad." The calm strength in Shade's voice eased something within her.

"I see."

What did her mother see? Did she see things the same as others did? Ever since being hit on the head by the Fresnel light, the item which somehow managed to break not only its C clamp but also a safety strap, Ashlynn had seen life in a different manner. Her mother had never been a kind person, but she had never realized how rude, arrogant, and downright unlikable she was.

Shade thanked the waiter before digging into the exquisite salad which had been brought out for him. "What I would do for some chicken. But I understand it's off the menu for the foreseeable future. Your sessions this morning, were they helpful?"

"Wonderful. Lakshmi is gifted in the art of massage." And she had been. It wasn't the young woman's fault her mother ruined her mood.

Shade faced her mother. "And you, Mrs. Stone? Did you have successful sessions this morning?"

"I had meditation, a stupider thing I've never heard of. A complete waste of time, in my opinion. As are most things on this island. But, as I'm stuck here for six more days, I shall make the best of it."

"I find meditation centers me. Interesting you are unable to find the benefits from such a simple thing as being with yourself."

Ashlynn almost choked on her food, which brought her mother's attention straight back to her and her empty plate. "How much have you eaten?"

"Enough." Yes, over the last four months she'd put on weight. A lot of weight. Before, she'd eaten next to nothing but rabbit food and employed all the model tricks to stay thin. Now she could barely work out because of the pain. She found simple enjoyment in eating. She didn't find solace in food but in the sustainable nutrients she had lacked for so long.

"May I say, you are far more appealing than the woman I remember form the billboard. Even with the small scar, your beauty is always there," Shade said between bites.

"She's the size of a car."

Shade stood up and leaned over the table. "I do not understand this need in you to belittle and destroy your children. You lost one daughter. If you want to lose another, keep this up. But you will find the upcoming years are cold, lonely, and unkind. You are about to be a grandmother. Perhaps that should give you food for thought."

"Mrs. Stone, Cemil is waiting for you in the yoga room," Sage said, eyeing Shade.

When her mother got up and left without another word, Ashlynn sat amazed. No one spoke to her that way, no one she knew of, anyway. The people in her mother's circles were afraid to say anything, scared the wrong word would put them in the bad social sphere. But Shade's concern had been for Ashlynn.

"My apologies, Sage," he said. "It is not my place to school your guests."

"You may school Mrs. Stone all you wish. But be careful she doesn't affect you." Without a pause, she continued, "Ashlynn, drink your shake. It will help. The kitchen has been instructed to keep chocolate off the menu for you. Not because of your waistline but because it might be a trigger to your headaches. There are lots of chocolate-free desserts for you, here."

The choice between the chocolate cake from last night and her headaches might be a toss-up. The cake had been divine. "Sage, where might I find my sister?"

"I believe she's with Serena this afternoon. Myron can tell you where she is and give you directions."

"I can take you to her," Shade said, pushing his plate away and standing up.

Sage smiled. "Excellent. Keep those glasses on. They might be awkward, but we need to gauge if they're working."

Ashlynn managed a weak smile. "I will thank you."

They walked out of the dining room in silence. She was unsure what to say to a man who stood up for her one minute, talked about speaking to souls another, and was so handsome it made her head spin and butterflies churn in her stomach. That said something. All the men on the island were a modeling agent's wet dream. But this one did things to her no man ever had. It both terrified and excited her. As they approach the front desk, Myron, who now wore Tonga's name tag, smiled. Before she could ask or question the purple-haired woman, she stated, "The lagoon. And you have a second session with Lakshmi this afternoon at four seeing as the first one was ruined by a certain lunch companion."

Uncertain how to react to either of those two things, she thanked her.

"Think nothing of it." She flipped a card. "Could

you ask Dana what she would like for lunch? The first tray Cherry sent down went untouched. Reese is hoping he will have better luck with the next one."

"Her appetite changes on a dime," Shade supplied. "I understand it's normal pregnant mama stuff. Most just don't have the luxury of an entire staff to cater to them."

"If only she would let us do that," Myron said. "Stubborn woman can't seem to sit back and let us pamper her."

"My sister's not really the pampered type." Of course she had never been given the opportunity to be.

"Oh," Myron exclaimed, dropping a card on the pile. "Oh my...have you told her?"

"Told her what?" Shade asked, but then glanced down at the three of clubs and nodded. They had both lost their marbles. "Yes, we discussed it this morning. But I don't think it's been made public knowledge yet."

"Mum's the word." The woman chuckled. "I'm so funny."

Shade shook his head at the bad pun but laughed, indicating the open double doors allowing the fresh breeze in. "Shall we?"

Ashlynn nodded and took a stabilizing breath. She hadn't walked out into the sun yet with her glasses and was unsure of how they would work and if they would help. He waited as if sensing her hesitation. "Do you want to ride or walk?"

"Let's walk." The view, though strange and not very pretty, offered no pain. The urge to stretch and get a bit of exercise overrode any other hesitation. He offered her his arm for support and, relieved, she took it. "Is the lagoon far?"

"About fifteen minutes, depending on how fast we walk. Her cabin is right on the beach, so should you need some darkness you can find it there."

She stumbled on the uneven path, and Shade pulled her tighter against him. For the first few minutes, they walked in peace, him allowing her the time she needed to focus and get her bearings. Cyrus had been right—once she got used to it, the shapes had begun to form images. "I get the impression you aren't a guest here yet aren't staff either."

"I am an outside...consultant. A friend of the Rowan family and of Rekkus."

"How can this place help me when everything else has failed?" She hadn't realized she'd voiced the question until Shade stopped and faced her. He pulled her into his arms as if it were his right, and even knowing all she did about him, she let him. Perhaps her defenses were down since Sage so motherly held her last night, or perhaps she craved human touch. But it felt so right to be there within the circle of his arms. He might be crazy, but he wasn't dangerous, she recognized he would never hurt her. Sage would never allow her to wonder off with anyone who would harm her. But perhaps she overthought. He had a strange if not sexy accent, and, perhaps, like Cyrus insisted, he could read people. Didn't everyone read people one way or another, some more adept than others? Police read suspects all the time, as did modeling agents.

The longer they stayed there locked in one another's arms, the more she wanted to stay. His earthy scent filled her senses, making her knees weak, and didn't want to contemplate the unsettling tingle between her legs. When Shade pulled back enough to lower his head and brush his lips against hers, she didn't stop him. It had been inevitable, and she welcomed the soft touch as she would an old friend.

She melted into him, loving the feel of his arms around her. She felt safe and protected. Desire, she had from others before, but protection was new. When his tongue passed her teeth, she moaned and embraced the sweet gentleness in the kiss.

He pulled back, rubbing his thumb over her bottom lip. "Come on, let's walk. You stop when you need to."

They walked in companionable silence. She loved how he didn't seem interested in her modeling career. How long had it been since someone hadn't harped on her about what it must be like to be a model, or, since her accident, how it must suck to have lost it all. But she didn't feel like she lost anything, and, by the time they came over the hill and she could see the lagoon, she had almost forgotten about the scar on her face, the funky glasses she wore, or the almost-constant pain in her skull. Her thoughts stayed on the gentle touch of their fingers.

"Back again, Shade." Two tall, bulky, and, yes, sexy-as-hell men, dressed in the security uniform of black jeans, a black skintight T-shirt, and black combat boots approached them.

"Juneau, we are here to see Dana."

"You have clearance. I need to check about Miss Stone," Juneau said matter of fact.

"I'm her sister, why the hell would I need clearance?" What the fuck?

"Give me one second please." The man tapped on the earpiece. "Rekkus, this is Juneau, come in."

"Are you kidding me?" she demanded.

Shade lifted a single digit to her lips.

"Hi, Cyrus.... No, she's fine. Still in the lagoon.... No Rekkus doesn't need to come back, Miss Stone is here to see her sister.... You don't want to check with the big guy? Your skin, not mine." The man smiled at them both. "Go on down."

She took two steps past them before turning on Shade. "Did I really have to get permission to see my sister?"

"Rekkus has his reasons."

"Is this an all-the-time thing or a way of keeping my mother away from her?" Somehow, though creepy and controlling, she could understand that reasoning.

"Though it would be a great thing to keep your mother away from all human beings at any given time, no, this is a regular thing on the island."

"Are you fucking kidding me? How much more possessive can the man get?"

"Don't ask questions you don't want the answers to."

Shade making light of the situations made Ashlynn angrier. Couldn't any of them see what was going on? Dana had become a virtual prisoner. Though she doubted anyone on the island would put up with physical abuse, would they stop her from leaving if Rekkus said she had to stay? They all clearly kowtowed to the man as if he were some king, or worse, some god.

"You're getting yourself worked up. Talking with your sister might put whatever fears you have at rest." He indicated her sister swimming with Serena. "I'll leave you to enjoy your visit. Perhaps I will see you at dinner."

He knew damned well he would see her at

dinner, and she almost said so, but because he couldn't see what went on with Rekkus and Dana didn't mean she had the right to be rude to someone who had been nothing but kind to her. So, she thanked him and waved when her sister noticed her presence.

Dana waved back and ambled out of the water, grabbing a towel from one of the many lounge chairs scattered on the white sandy beach. "What a lovely treat."

Ashlynn smiled at the genuine joy she heard in her sister's voice. She didn't know how her sister could be happy to see her when she hadn't stood up for her after Dana's botched marriage attempt to Frank Green. When her sister had needed her most, she hid behind her mother like a coward, unable to stand against her. "I didn't interrupt you, did I?"

"Not at all. Serena helped me to relax and she has other work to do, though she is too nice to say so." Dana pulled a sundress over her head before indicating they go inside. They walked to the open-air cabin, a perfect fit for her down-to-earth sister. "Can I get you something to drink? All I have is cucumber water, but I can make a call, and believe me, they will be down with whatever I want. I look forward to the day when they tell me to get it my damned self."

Somehow, Ashlynn didn't think that day would ever come. "Water would be great."

They both remained silent, the awkward silence that sits when things need to be said but you don't know where to start. Taking a deep breath and steadying herself, Ashlynn bit the proverbial bullet. "I've been a lousy sister."

Dana paused in the act of putting the water glass

on the table and took a deep breath, too. She sat as gracefully as a woman carrying twins can beside her. "No, we have an awful mother. There is a difference."

"I should have stood by you, supported you, done something."

"What? Ever since you were a baby, she punished you for anything that might make our relationship strong. She did everything she could to keep us on separate sides of the field. We weren't even allowed in each other's rooms."

"I don't remember that."

"You were young. By the time you were old enough to remember, it was second nature for us to stay apart. I never blamed you, might have been jealous of your perfect body, hair, and complexion from time to time, but I always loved you." Dana reached out and grabbed her sister's hand. "I always hoped somewhere deep inside you would love me, too."

Ashlynn grimaced. She had, and somehow it took being hit on the head with a fourteen-pound lamp to find the part of her hiding her emotion and humanity. "Why didn't Dad ever stand up for us?"

"He worked so much I don't think he saw the problems until it was too late. He had his residency when you were little. Rarely home, no life to speak of, and she never showed how hateful she could be around him." Dana leaned back, rubbing her belly. "Enough about the past. How are you feeling?"

"Better. Sage is a miracle worker. She could make a fortune on the mainland."

"She is amazing. They all are here."

"You seem content and happy here. Are you? Are you really?" Ashlynn asked, hoping it would nudge Dana into opening up about her marriage.

"I am." She smiled on a sigh. "For the most part."

"What is it, please tell me. I know we haven't been close, but I hope we can be," Ashlynn pleaded and prayed her sister could find the strength to speak up if she needed to.

Dana hesitated. "Please don't get me wrong. I'm happy. I'm getting a little nervous, though."

"The babies?"

"I should have three weeks according to everyone else, but something inside tells me they are coming next week." Dana stood and started to pace. "I can't articulate how I know, I just know. And I'm not sure I can do this. Labor, motherhood.... What if I turn out like our mother? What if...?"

"Now you're being crazy. You are nothing like her at all. But of course you are nervous. I mean, two babies...."

"Three!" her sister shrieked. "Shade found the third this morning."

Not touching that one, not yet. Instead, she remained calm, even if, inside, she screamed to get her to a safe hospital. "Do multiples run in Rekkus' family?"

"Twins, yes, not triplets."

"Dana, come back to the city with us on Saturday. I'm sure Dad can get you set up with an associate even this late in your pregnancy. You should be in a hospital, not on this island so far from medical help."

"It's not so easy."

"If it's the money...."

"It's not the money at all. Mother dearest could find nothing wrong with Rekkus' bank statement, if I showed it to her, no matter how hard she tried. Even if I could go, he won't leave the island."

"So, because he won't leave, you have to stay and endanger your and the babies' lives."

"There is so much more to it."

"What excuses are you going to come up with next? He's a bully and I am worried."

"Worried how?" Dana stopped in her tracks, a shocked bewilderment crossing her face.

"How long had you known him when you got married? What, a week, two at most? A courier brought our parents cash to repay their expenses for your cancelled wedding. Were you aware he had the amount down to the penny? Including items you didn't have any clue about. How did he know, Dana? He has a team of, albeit handsome, scary goons who follow his every command."

"He is head of security. It's their job."

"Security here is tighter than at the White House. I know. I attended a White House Christmas party. This is not normal." She threw her hands up.

"The island isn't exactly normal."

"If I brought out a checklist of early signs of controlling and abusive husbands, I could check off every item on the list for you."

"What?"

"Overprotective, possessive to the extreme, quick trigger temper, and—"

"Stop right there." Dana pointed at Ashlynn, her voice cracking. "He loves me. Yes, he is worried. What father isn't when his children are this close to birth?"

"Then he would make sure you had the best possible care."

"I do, and I'm pregnant, not sick."

"But surely with more than one—"

"And how have the hospitals been helping you?"

Ashlynn opened her mouth to respond then shrugged. "I hate it when you do that."

"Stop pouting. I promise you there is no way any man would be allowed to abuse me. Do you believe the Rowans would put up with him harming me? Let's change the subject and talk about you. What are your plans? Have you thought about extending your stay here?"

"I think they want me, Mom, and Dad off the island as soon as the boat gets here."

Calm again, Dana took a sip of her water as she eased down into the chair. "You and Dad are welcome to stay, all you have to do is say the word and I'll make it happen."

Some of the tension within her eased. "Another week might be nice."

"Good, I'll talk with Myron. How is your head?"

She took a second to assess. "Surprisingly better today."

"I heard last night was bad."

She nodded. "Shade got me the help I needed before it was out of control."

"Rekkus has a lot of respect for the man, and respect isn't something easy to come by with my hubby."

Ashlynn bit her lip, wondering how to broach her biggest concern about Shade. "He told me he could read souls."

"He can."

Ashlynn snorted. "Oh, please."

"You need to open your mind a bit, oh sister mine. Tell me about these glasses."

Ashlynn had forgotten about them. "They are

hideous and mother hates them, which makes me love them even more."

Through the open window drifted the voices of approaching men. Dana stood, a spark of excitement entering her dark eyes. Something almost magical in the way she couldn't wait to see her husband even after a few hours put Ashlynn's mind at ease at least a little.

"Give me a minute or two, Kaleb, and then we can go over your plans. Why don't you call Cyrus down to join us?" Rekkus walked by the open window, stopping to smile when his sight landed on Dana. Every ounce of his being screamed the love he had for her. He walked in, kissed his wife on the forehead, and reached for her almost-empty water glass. "How are you feeling, luv?"

"Better, between Serena and my sister, it's been a relaxing sort of day."

Returning a full glass to her, he brushed her hair from her cheek. "Good, and you have a message from the Haus."

"I don't know what or where I want to eat." She groaned, sitting back down. "I meant no insult to either Cherry or Reese. I am not hungry."

"I figured but I have to work with the teens today, so if you decide to walk up to the main building, please call someone to escort you. Juneau and Zander are working close by today if you need them."

"Yes, boss."

"Funny." He took a chug from his cup.

"I can come back after my next class and walk with you. It's so nice to be active again." She looked at her sister and grimaced. "Sorry."

"Not your fault I can only waddle a few feet in an

hour. It's his." She indicated the man in the kitchen.

"You are just full of jokes today," Rekkus seemed to purr.

"So, do you need to let your guard dogs know I'm coming through the barriers, or did I get the all-access pass," Ashlynn joked but realized almost immediately this wasn't a joking matter.

The room grew icy, as if an arctic blast moved through the area. Rekkus paused mid-gulp, and Dana bolted out of her seat like a woman about to jump hurdles in boot camp, not give birth in a few weeks. Rekkus said a few words in another language, and it didn't take much to realize the words weren't the kind used in mixed company.

"Don't you dare curse at me." If Dana could breathe fire, she would.

"Crap on a cracker. I cursed the universe, not anyone in particular."

"Shut up. What guards, Rekkus?" When he didn't answer, she turned on Ashlynn. "Where are the guards?"

Ashlynn shrugged, figuring out an escape plan. She had unearthed a series of land mines and didn't know how to get around them. She met Rekkus' golden gaze, and he inclined his head. Taking a deep breath, she said, "There are two guards at the top of the hill."

Rekkus closed his eyes, clenching his jaw as he gripped the countertop. Dana glared at him. "Why the hell do you have guards posted up there?"

"Luv."

"Don't you luv me." Dana folded her arms. When they rested on her belly, it seemed to enrage her more so she settled for fisting her hands at her sides.

"Rekkus. I'm sorry. I had no idea."

Rekkus' focus never left Dana. "Not your fault completely."

"It's not her fault at all." Dana's voice reached a higher octave.

"Maybe I should leave you two alone." Ashlynn got to her feet.

Rekkus looked at her, stunned. A glance clearly saying, You're not leaving me alone with this crazy woman, are you? crossed his face. "Chicken."

Ashlynn shifted toward the exit.

"Ashlynn, leave." Dana threw her arm out toward the open door.

"Oh, thank god."

Rekkus, stuck with no way out, yelled after her, "Perhaps you should check who is watching before you start another snogging session with Shade on the path."

"What?" Dana blinked at her sister. "You made out with Shade?"

"I.... We didn't do much—" Ashlynn began.

"To be fair, Dana, we—" Rekkus tried to intercede.

"I told you to shut up." She turned on him before glaring at her sister. "Why do I hear this from him?"

"Well, it was just a small kiss."

Dana stared between the two of them in utter disbelief. Rekkus mouthed, You'd better run now. He didn't have to tell her twice. She ran out the door as quick as her feet could take her, and although the window remained wide open and large enough for even Dana in her present state to emerge from, she breathed a sigh of relief when the door closed behind her.

A chuckle from the other cabin caught her

attention. Kaleb, Serena's husband, sat on his own porch eating popcorn and watching the cabin with rapt interest and quite a bit of satisfaction.

"Are you honestly eating popcorn?"

"Best entertainment on the island, these two, when they get into it." He held out the bowl and, when she shook her head, he shrugged, popping a few more kernels into his mouth. "It doesn't happen a lot, but when it does, wooo, baby."

"You find this amusing?"

He smiled. "Oh hell, yeah."

"When did we discuss this?" Dana's shriek came through the open window.

"We agreed to more security after the attack on the beach." Rekkus remained calm and rational.

Ashlynn was about to ask what attack, but Kaleb shushed her.

"No we didn't," Dana said.

"You didn't argue," Rekkus said as if that argument would work. Stupid man.

"I thought you were dying."

Ashlynn indicated the house of chaos. "How is this funny?"

"If it makes Rekkus squirm, even for a moment, it brings a little joy into all our lives. He likes things orderly; he likes to be in charge. Okay, you figured that one out on your own. But Dana is definitely in charge of their relationship. She doesn't follow his commands. She does what she wants, sometimes without thinking it through, and it makes him crazy."

Rekkus stormed out, slamming the door so hard behind him Ashlynn swore the earth shook. Glancing up, she noticed a thunder cloud forming above the house. "That's odd."

"Yeah, that's been happening a lot lately. I need to ask Sarka about it, but I have been delaying it as long as possible. Sarka has an uglier temper than Rekkus." Kaleb left the bowl on the table beside him, brushed the butter off on his jeans, and stood.

"And I am going to take a nap because I want to, not because you think I need one," Dana yelled.

Rekkus reached his hand up in the air in time to catch the first of three apples flung at the back of his head. He never flinched catching each one in succession, and with great gentleness he laid the apples on the outside table under the window.

"You tell the Rowans not to come near me today."

Rekkus put a palm up, stopping the two who were about to come around the corner. Sage with an 'O' forming on her lips and Cyrus who took on the appearance of a kid who couldn't wait to open a present his curiosity piqued. Rekkus pointed. "You, Kaleb, up at the training grounds in fifteen and bring reinforcements."

As Rekkus stormed off, Cyrus crept around the house, staying out of the line of sight of the window. "I suggest you bring more than a few, and make one of them the bear."

Kaleb made a few hand gestures toward the tree line before grabbing one last handful of popcorn. In a moment, three more men strode onto the beach. They nodded before heading back into the woods.

"How many in total are watching Dana?"

"After what just happened, don't you think ignorance might be bliss?" Kaleb asked.

Ashlynn considered the quiet house where the rain cloud had somewhat cleared. Whatever fears she had about her brother-in-law were laid to rest.

Although he might like control, he didn't seem to have it where her sister was involved. She ruled their roost.

"Can someone tell me what the hell is happening? Dana seemed perfectly happy when I left with Rekkus two hours ago," Cyrus whispered in a rather loud voice.

"She found out about the guards," Serena said as she came out of the cabin and retrieved the popcorn bowl. "I told you she would."

Cyrus winced. "All of them?"

All of them? How many guards did one pregnant woman need?

"I think the two up the hill." Kaleb kissed his wife and said, "I'm going to get my ass kicked. See everyone at dinner. Ashlynn, always a pleasure."

Ashlynn vowed to play dumb when it came to anything involving her sister and her husband, and, if asked anything, she would plead the fifth.

Cyrus positioned a hand on the small of her back. "Come on, troublemaker. Let's get you to your acupuncture session."

***

Trying to keep his mind off a certain tall brunette with legs that went on for days proved to be impossible even with all the activity going on within the Haus. Cemil, having dealt with Mrs. Stone, had a migraine bordering on being complex. Everyone agreed Cemil would retreat to Shade's cottage, and Shade would assume his workload for the day. Which included escorting Mrs. Stone and her daughter who he had kissed this morning.

Having dropped off Cemil, who was in no way able to drive himself down to the cottage, Myron, the maniac driver who could give any Boston driver a run for their money, detoured by the training fields. Shade wasn't sure what they were training for, but it appeared to be "how to get your ass kicked by a were-tiger."

Returning to the Haus, Shade had a few minutes to spare before meeting with the senior Stone female. He decided to check in with Sage, whom he hadn't had much time to chat with since arriving on the island. He found her, as expected, in her herb-drying room behind the garden.

"Watch your head," Sage mumbled without turning. Didn't matter who entered. Unless they were Sage's size, they would hit their head on the low doorframe.

Rich fresh herbs assailed his senses. Most he recognized: lavender, chamomile, mint. Some he had never seen before. "What are all these on the back wall?"

They were stockpiling herbs. Sage smiled, a slight pink hue covering her cheeks. "Herbs to delay labor, herbs to induce labor, herbs to ease labor. We have every herb known to witch-kind to aid Dana when she gives birth. I might have overdone it a bit."

"Better to be prepared."

"Have a seat." She indicated a tall wooden stool in the corner of the room as she pulled some herbs from overhead. "Butterbur and feverfew, these along with the lemon-ginger beer I have brewing in the kitchen should ease Cemil's headaches."

If anyone could, it was Sage. Ever since the woman could walk, she'd gravitated to the herb gardens. Rumor had it she'd tinkered with her

93

mother's window herb garden before she could talk and created a potion which had saved her sister from a bad case of influenza.

The Rowans' powers had always been top-notch, and it had been no surprise when this generation showed their prowess. The Syndicate worried very little about the light ones who could do no harm. Sage worked to better life for those around her. Her heart and soul were as pure as a mountain spring. "Can we discuss Ashlynn Stone and her headaches?"

It seemed he couldn't get away from her today. "Yes. How can I help?"

"You know the old saying, having the sense knocked into you?"

"Yes."

"I think this might have been the case with her. According to Dana, this is not the Ashlynn most people know. She was, if not self-centered, then reserved, never going against the wishes of her mother. I would bet she was afraid, too. But the Ashlynn everyone describes is not the person I see, not, I believe, what her soul is."

"You believe her soul is in conflict."

"Perhaps, and perhaps it wasn't being hit in the head that rattled her. Maybe it was her mother's defection and abandonment showing her the true light of her mother's being. But I think if we can mend her soul we can lessen the headaches."

"I will do my best. But the oddities of the island are confusing to her, which is not helping her headaches. Perhaps you can talk with Dana and Rekkus and see if they might wish to let the cat out of the bag, so to speak."

"I don't think Dana is speaking to Rekkus at the

moment or to any Rowans for that matter, but when she does, I'll suggest it." Sage shrugged but didn't add more. "Can I ask you one more thing? Something that has weighed heavy on us since your arrival? Were you sent here to spy on us?"

Yes, the four, five if you wanted to count Rekkus, on the island posed a threat to the Syndicate, and everyone knew it. "I would never spy on you, Sage. I work for the Syndicate, but I am not their lackey or their mole. I'm here to assess the state of things with the cubs. Rekkus' volatile temper is as always a concern, but rebuilding of the streak is of the utmost importance to the Syndicate, thus their concern for Dana's safety."

"What did you find this morning when you met with them?" Sage carried a mortar and pestle past him.

Normally, he would have let Dana and Rekkus break the news, but, as the midwife, Sage had to be informed, and if Dana went into labor before she decided to speak to any of the siblings, it could be a dangerous situation. "I found a third cub."

"Three." Sage dropped the mortar and pestle on the floor. The bowl broke into three clean pieces while the handle rolled under a table. Shade moved to pick up the shards and then moved Sage to the stool he'd vacated. "Can they be safely birthed here?"

"There is no longer a choice. She is too far into the pregnancy to move her through the portals, and no one can say what effect the fog wall will have on the cubs. I suspect, as shifters have told us in the past, they have to fight the urge to shift when coming through it, the cubs would shift, and she cannot handle the cubs in tiger form. Her uterus isn't tough enough."

Sage wrung her hands fretting. "I don't think I can do this. With the impending full moon, they might be forced to shift. If anything happened to her...."

Shade gripped her hands, forcing his strength into her. Yes, there were dangers in any birth, more with a human carrying para babies. Add to that the moon's pull and they had a situation that could move out of control quickly, but Sage had powers she hadn't unlocked yet. She could do this. He knew that with all the certainty in his soul. "Would you doubt yourself if you didn't love Dana so much?"

"No."

"Remember, you are what the family needs and you have something no one else in the world has."

"What is that?"

"You have the tiger prince's trust."

Chapter Seven

Ashlynn took another bite of her pasta. Though the kitchen prepared only the most delicious food, it tasted like dust today. Everyone at her table picked at their food— clearly nothing resembling healing and relaxation had happened today.

Her mother's foul mood emanated from her in waves, but while Cyrus stood over Dana ready to pounce at anything negative directed toward her pregnant daughter, she didn't say a word. As if she couldn't be bothered with her general nastiness. Ashlynn's head ached, and all she craved was peace.

The all-too-familiar pang of guilt she associated with her sister washed over her afresh. She wished she had kept her mouth shut about the guards. Cyrus had explained the dynamics behind Rekkus and his overprotective nature. She'd shuddered at what happened to his family and about the attack on the island from some mob boss who took Dana hostage to get his runaway wife back.

What husband wouldn't feel protective under those circumstances? Dana glanced longingly at the door then back at her plate before pushing the food around with her fork. Her actions left the kitchen staff fretting on the edges of the room. The ripple effect grew in momentum. Her dad's warm touch on her shoulder brought her from her musings. Whatever sessions he did today left him refreshed and younger in appearance than in years, a stark contrast to her mother who seemed to have aged a decade in two days.

"What class do you have tonight?" He sat down and placed his napkin in his lap.

"Meditation with Cemil." She forced a smile she didn't feel.

"Cemil came down with a migraine. A guy can only deal with nastiness for so long before his head implodes." Although Cyrus directed his comment at Ashlynn, his eyes never wavered from her mother's. Dana gaped, and, for the first time since the blowout earlier, she addressed one of the Rowans. "Cemil spent the whole day with her? His soul can't deal with such ugliness."

"Dana, calm down." Cyrus crouched next to Dana, rubbing her arm. "Cemil would be distraught if he thought for a moment he caused you any distress. He has suffered these headaches all his life. He will be right as rain after his night at one of the more remote cabins. Shadedor is taking over his classes tonight. And maybe tomorrow."

Ashlynn blushed. Dana bit her lip and gave a cheeky grin. "So, Shade will be teaching Ash here how to relax? Now, that is interesting."

Heat rushed through Ashlynn as she attempted to deflect the attention from her, but Cyrus chuckled. "Do you have the hots for Shade? And here I thought you wanted me."

Ashlynn's chin shot up. "It's not.... I mean we....
I....."

Cyrus sat beside her. "Calm down, honey, I was
teasing."

Cyrus's uncertainty left her floundering, but
when Shade came near, her libido went haywire and
she wanted to do things to the man that might be
illegal in some states. A hush came over the table.
Standing there in a sea of ripped shirts and muddy
faces were ten men who looked to have been having
better days.

"Kaleb," Dana whispered.

"Stay right where you are, Dana, and, yes, it's
worse than it appears." He searched the room. "Has
anyone seen my wife?"

"Not tonight, but you might find her at the hot
spring, waiting for you." Cyrus peered at Kaleb's
swollen eye. "Rekkus doesn't usually go for the face."

"Well, this wasn't Rekkus. We decided to attack
him all at once. There's a reason they don't do it in
the movies," Kaleb grumbled, jerking his thumb at
the men behind him. "This is thanks to one of their
elbows."

"It's a beaut, for sure," one of the men mumbled,
cracking his neck.

Dana touched Kaleb's arm. "Kaleb."

"It's okay. I shouldn't have laughed. I know
better." He smiled then palmed his swollen jaw. "But
do keep in mind over the next week or two we, your
husband's staff, are on your side. Could you just let us
watch over you? Who is it hurting?"

She put her head in her hands. "I am so sorry."

"So am I." Everyone got quiet and turned as
Rekkus strolled in. Other than a little mud on his
boots and a scratch on his forehead, he showed no

signs of the melee the others described.

"May I be dismissed?" Kaleb asked.

Rekkus nodded and waved off the rest of the men as well.

He bent to her and she buried her face in his chest. "I should have told you. But for me to function, I have to know you are safe. Otherwise, I won't get anything done. Please understand I can't lose you, too."

"The guards can stay, if...."

"If?"

She peeked up at him. "If you take a birthing class with me tonight with Trixie."

At an animal-like growl from Rekkus, Ashlynn jumped in fright.

Cyrus grabbed her shoulder and squeezed. "It's okay."

"Knock it off, Rekkus." Dana pushed away from him. "This is nonnegotiable. Go take a shower because you stink. I'll have the kitchen make you a sandwich before you meet me outside by the cliffs for our class."

"Fine." He glared at Cyrus, daring him to say something—anything, before leaving the room.

"Well played, Dana," Cyrus said with a chuckle.

"And you, Cyrus. Don't think I haven't realized you were in on this from the very beginning. You two seem to have one brain between you and, unfortunately, the one doing the talking is never the one with the brain."

"Dana, wait—"

"No, you wait. You will fill in for Rekkus until he gets back from his shower."

"Yes, well, childbirth class is for couples. Not

couples and their best friend." Cyrus shifted from one foot then the other, much like a little boy trying to get out of doing an unwanted chore.

"You and Rekkus are joined at the hip. When has being a couple ever kept you from anything?" Dana demanded. "You practically live in our living room. Tell me when was the last time you and my mate went more than a couple of hours without talking?"

Cyrus seemed to think about it then smirked. "How about when those babies were conceived?"

"Check and mate," Sage said, coming from behind them. "Cyrus, take Mama here to Trixie and, yes, you do need to stay until Rekkus gets there."

"But I don't want to." He pouted, and Ashlynn wondered if he would stomp his foot as well.

"I don't care." Sage looked from Dana to the uneaten food on her plate. "A dinner tray will be left in your cottage for you after your class. Now on your way, Cyrus. I want to chat with Ashlynn before Shade gets here."

Cyrus rolled his eyes but, in the end, did as he was told. The ladies of the island did seem to have full control of the men. But, at the moment, everyone focused on Dana and her babies. Perhaps the city with all its medical equipment might not compare to the island's warmth, caring, and, above all, love.

"What bothers you, Ashlynn?"

"I suppose saying nothing wouldn't float with you?"

"Not a chance."

"I didn't think so." She paused to figure out the best words to avoid being insulting. "I worry that perhaps Dana needs to be in a more clinical setting."

"Would it make you feel better if I told you, with the exception of maybe Rekkus, we all have felt the same way at some point during her pregnancy. But when I'm not doubting my own abilities, I know this is where she needs to be." She stood. "Come, let me show you something."

"Time to let the cat out of the bag?" Shade asked, coming toward them.

"One of them and, once I talk with Rekkus, perhaps a second."

Shade lowered his head in agreement. "May I join you for this one?"

"How many cats are in bags around here?" Ashlynn asked, confused by the conversations swirling around her.

"More and more every day." Sage sighed.

They walked down the hall to the elevator Ashlynn couldn't use. Sage pressed the button and waited. As the lift opened, they moved in and Ashlynn felt like something in her life would be changing tonight.

"Stop worrying. This will put your mind at ease." Shade seemed so sure, but Ashlynn didn't believe him.

When they exited, Ashlynn noticed a woman dressed in white seated at a desk in the hallway. "Nurse Janis, this is Ashlynn, Dana's sister. Should the need arise, she is allowed up here."

The woman gave her a warm smile. "Nice to meet you, Ashlynn. Dr. Belmonte is down the hall in his office." As they strolled past, the woman lifted a pencil and poised it over a book of crossword puzzles. Sage opened a door at the end of the empty hallway. "We showed this to your father earlier."

She ushered Ashlynn into an immaculate operating room. Lots of shiny instruments, gleaming white walls and floors, and a new feel to everything. "Has Dana seen this?"

"Once. She prefers to think about natural childbirth, but Rekkus wanted to make sure, should the need arise, we could take care of her and the babies. We have a full staff on call."

"So they are here in case Dana needs them," Shade assured.

"That seems like a lot of expense for just in case."

"Your brother-in-law can afford it. But we thought the knowledge would help you breathe a little better."

"It does. Thank you."

"It did your father, too." Sage smiled, and the nurse came around the corner.

"Sage, Myron phoned. Ms. Silverstein needs you." Nurse Janis indicated the direction they had come in with a flick of her head.

"If you two would excuse me?"

"Is there anything else you want to see up here?" Shade asked.

She shook her head, still in shock at what she saw. "No. That's it for now."

Shade waved her ahead of him down the hallway to the elevator. He kept a wide distance between them. While she longed for him to touch her or be close, he seemed to be pulling away. Of course, he would be conducting her class later. Maybe he didn't want to blur the lines between staff and guest.

Once they were outside, he spoke. "We have our choice of locations tonight. We can head to the lake, into the apple orchard, or, if you prefer, the yoga room. I believe the cliff area is being used by Trixie for childbirth classes."

"How about the lake? I haven't been there yet."

She estimated they had thirty minutes of light left, and she wanted to be outside as long as possible. Once the light failed her, ability to see would diminish as well.

He walked. This morning, he had been right next to her, and there had been constant contact. Now they would appear to anyone passing to be complete strangers. "You want to tell me what is going on?"

"We are attempting to remove all stress from your life in hopes of easing the headaches."

"No, with you. If you would prefer to be elsewhere, I can go back to my room and lie down."

He stopped. "There is nowhere I would rather be."

"Then why are you acting like I have the plague? Was it the kiss earlier?"

"I overstepped my boundaries this morning. I should not have done so."

"Do you regret it?"

"I am assisting the staff here in your healing. It is inappropriate for me to come on to you."

"Are you on staff here?"

"No."

"That settles it." She smiled. Closing the distance between them, she wrapped her arms around his neck. "I do not know what is going on, but I do know my pain and fears ease when you are near. I don't claim to understand how you discern all you do, but I am starting to see things here aren't always black and white, and sometimes I have to have faith and trust."

After a brief second of him standing as still as a statue and her wondering if she read too much into this morning's embrace, he relaxed. His arms snaked around her, pulling her against his hard body. His mouth came down on hers begging her to open for him, demanding she submit to his kiss. She might have started this dance, but he would damned well be leading it.

Lifting her off her feet, he moved them both off the main path and into the cover of the trees. Not a great hiding place, but it might prevent another ragging from Rekkus. His lips worked their way over her cheek to the soft spot under her earlobe. "I have been overrun by images of you in my arms all day."

"I, on the other hand, got funny looks from all the staff for, I quote, 'snogging' with you."

He pulled back, gazing into her eyes and grinned. "I'll make it up to you."

"Not tonight you won't, Romeo." Sarka stood on the path staring at them both with her hands on her hips. "I've been asked to tell you the other cat is about to come out of the bag, whatever the hell that means. Sage assured me you would understand."

"Thank you, Sarka."

"By the way, she has a room. Try using it." Sarka turned on her heel and wandered off.

"How can she be related to the other three?"

"Hard to believe, isn't it?" He smiled, fixed Ashlynn's clothes so it didn't appear she had been accosted, and, hand in hand, they walked down toward the beach.

Ashlynn's steps slowed as they came to the top of the hill leading down to the lagoon. "You already know what is about to be said, don't you?"

Shade nodded. "I do."

"Can you tell me?"

He pulled her into his arms, ascertaining what she needed before she did. "It's not my secret to tell, and, if I told you, I don't think you would believe me anyway."

"Is it bad?"

"No, just different." With an encouraging nudge, he urged her down the trail. "Come on." To her surprise, her father waited for them, and no surprise her mother was nowhere to be found. Rekkus made a great number of concessions where Ashlynn and her father were concerned but stood unwavering regarding her mother. Rekkus protected Dana, but he couldn't protect his wife from words thrown at her. No one could, and sometimes words hurt worse than fists.

"Hey, glad you came." Dana's smile didn't hide her nervousness.

"Apparently, you have something to share with us. Something more important than your birthing class?"

"I...we do." Dana peered over her shoulder at her bedroom door. "We will head back to class in a bit."

Rekkus came out of the bedroom, naked as a jaybird. Awe of his perfect chiseled body turned to an ick factor at seeing her brother-in-law naked.

Dana blushed. "Rekkus!"

"I can't do this when I am dressed," he stated as if he made all the sense in the world.

"You could have worn a towel." She threw a pillow at him, as nervous as Ashlynn had ever seen her. "There is something we need to tell you, well, show you. I don't know how to...."

"Baby, I got this." A second later, he disappeared, and in his place stood a massive tiger no color she had ever seen in nature. Black with silver stripes.

Their dad slumped onto the arm of the chair he had been standing near, gaping at the cat.

Ashlynn knew she hallucinated. "Yeah, that didn't just happen."

"Are you kidding me?" Dana threw her hands up in the air.

Then Rekkus returned. "Well, your way wasn't working."

"Is that your idea of being subtle?" Shade asked.

"Do they know? Yes. Object achieved," Rekkus said as if they were talking about the weather and he wasn't again naked.

"Yes, but you could have had them sit down first or given them some warning." Dana tried to shove her husband out of view.

The room spun. Ashlynn pulled off her glasses to stabilize her life. "That didn't just happen."

Rekkus shrugged. "I can do it again if you need me to."

Ashlynn and her dad chorused, "No."

She closed her eyes, her world turned, and the next thing she knew she lay horizontal on the sofa, Shade sitting next to her, patting her hand, and her sister hovering. Rekkus—fully dressed—brought her a glass of water. "At least the Stone sisters handle my shifting the same."

"Excuse me?" Ashlynn asked.

Dana giggled. "I passed out, too."

"Oh?" She sat up. "Where is Dad?"

"He needed some air," Dana said, pointing out the window at their father silhouetted against the setting sun. "Maybe this wasn't the best idea."

"No, it's better this way." Why had she said that? She couldn't think. Someone turning into an animal was something of myths, fairy tales, and horror films. "So, are you carrying tigers?"

"She is carrying babies," Sage said with a smile.

"But now you know why she can't deliver anywhere else."

Ashlynn nodded. "Um, I'm not feeling great. Do you think we could talk about this more in the morning when it's had time to settle in."

Dana bit her nail and nodded.

"All I care about is your happiness, Dana. His being a tiger is a bit weird, but who am I to say anything?" I'd give anything for someone to love me like he loves you.

***

Shade led Ashlynn out of the house after a brief series of good-byes and assuring a hormonal sister everything was fine. They took Sage's cart as Shade didn't believe Ashlynn couldn't make the fifteen-minute walk. The shock of seeing someone shift into an animal would be hard for anyone. The slow, tense drive seemed never ending. Ashlynn sat silent, staring straight ahead. He didn't blame her for needing time to absorb the new reality they'd shown her. Once she did, she'd have questions, and he wanted to be the one to answer them for her.

That damned Rekkus had very little empathy for humans. Amazing the Fates found one who could put up with him.

Shade parked the golf cart and waited for Ashlynn to move or speak. Finally, she mumbled, "Can I beg a favor?"

"Anything in my power to give you."

"Will you stay in my room tonight? Keep me company? I just don't want to be alone. And, when I am with you, I don't feel the pain so strongly."

"I would be happy to stay with you. Let me grab my bag, and then we can head to your room."

She smiled at Myron, who asked how it went. Ashlynn just continued to smile.

"That well, huh?" Myron tapped a card on the desk.

"He was very naked."

"'Ah, Kitty tends to like the naked part. Nice for us, too."

Shade reached into the office and grabbed his bag he had left there earlier. Throwing it over his back, he followed Ashlynn to the elevators. "You have to press the button. It won't let me."

"Won't let you?"

Shade debated explaining the elevators and how they worked but decided to keep this simple. "I am not a guest, nor am I staff."

"Ah."

Once in her room Ashlynn told him to make himself at home while she changed. A few minutes later, she came out dressed in a long T-shirt. "Can you hold me, please? I feel like my world is altered, somehow, and will never be the same. He isn't even my husband, but I feel unsure. Scared."

Shade kicked off his shoes and took her hand. Settling her on the bed, he lay behind her and pulled the blanket over them both. Even though this had to happen, he wished he could have sheltered her from it. Suddenly, everything in Rekkus' overprotective behavior toward Dana made sense. And, as the thought hit, his ability to read Ashlynn's soul disappeared.

Ah hell. What a time for the Fates to find his mate.

Chapter Eight

"Excuse me?" Rekkus demanded, storming out of his office. Angry did not begin to explain the emotions running through the other man at the moment.

"The three are expecting you and Shade." Myron remained behind her desk, out of reach of Rekkus and his temper.

"No." Rekkus began to pace, never a good sign. "No."

"Rekkus, you are going to wake the entire building. Keep your voice down."

"Myron, I am not leaving this island." He slammed his fist into the receptionist's table.

Shade decided to step in. "You have to."

Rekkus spun toward him. "How long have you known about this?"

"I found out right before you did," Shade said, as surprised though not as irate as the tiger. "Listen, we have thirty minutes until sunrise when the portal opens. I suggest you inform Dana about what is going on."

Myron murmured, "It's safe. The babies aren't

coming today."

"I thought you weren't going to read the babies."

"I'm not. I am reading you." She threw the king of clubs at him. "Shall I wake Cyrus and tell him to get ready?"

"Cyrus can't come," Shade said. Cyrus' safety remained here. Even without Rekkus, the safeguards put in place would protect him for the twelve hours they would be gone.

"The hell he can't. If I leave, so does he. Myron, call Kaleb. Wake him up. I need him up here now. Now means five minutes ago. I will fill him in once I have talked with Dana. And get Cyrus and Sarka."

"I'm up," Sarka muttered, cradling a cup of coffee and heading into her office.

"Is it wise, Myron?" Shade quieted his voice which made no sense even as he did it because Rekkus could hear almost everything said on the island no matter where he was.

"The safest place for Cyrus is always with Rekkus, as you know. You were the one who fought so hard to get Rekkus to take the position as his bodyguard all those years ago." Myron knew information no one else did.

She made her calls, and as the players arrived, the lobby and office area began to bustle with activity.

Sarka came out of the office. "Shade, will you be returning tonight?"

"I am planning to." With his soul mate on the island, he'd like to see them keep him away.

"Give me your palm." Shade held out his arm and flinched as Sarka drew blood with a knife. She forced his hand into a fist and collected the blood into a vial.

The ringing of the elevator caught his attention

before Cyrus appeared, yawning. "Do we have time for coffee?" He handed his sister a vial of blood before moving into her office.

"He had to use his own knife," Sarka said to no one in particular.

Dana, exhausted and in Rekkus' clothes, Kaleb rumpled, with shadows under his eyes, and Serena—as always gorgeous, smiling, and proving why people hated mermaids—entered from outside.

"Coffee is in the office," Myron offered.

"Oh goodie," Serena said.

Sarka shook her head, but, with a gentleness unlike her, said, "What are you doing out of bed, Dana?"

"Wanted to see the portal...seemed a good opportunity." She stifled a yawn and sat on the chair next to where her husband stood. She laid her head against his thigh and closed her eyes. Rekkus continued to chat with Kaleb, playing with Dana's hair. He held out his free hand without being asked and gave his blood.

"I'll be back in five minutes." Sarka disappeared into the first elevator.

"Can I get you something to eat?" Dana asked.

Rekkus shook his head. "No, we'll get something on the other side. Best to have an empty stomach when going through these things."

"How long has it been?" Dana stretched.

"Over five years." Rekkus smiled at her. "I'll be back at sunset."

"You'd better. We have our second birth class."

"How can I forget?" He helped her out of the chair and led her to a door at the far end of the hall. "Stay in the Haus while I'm gone. The bed in my office is freshly made up."

"I will. I think I'll hang with Sage and my sister today. Maybe find Cemil. He relaxes when he rubs my tummy, and it's the least I can do."

Rekkus brought his mouth close to her protruding belly and placed a gentle kiss there. "You three behave. Allow your mum some peace today."

"I have contacted one of our people in the capital. They'll spread the rumor your visit is to shop for baby things. This offers a good reason for you to leave the safety of the island." Myron handed him a list. "Should you have time, I suggest you buy an item or two from this."

Sarka approached a few minutes later. "As soon as you are through, I'll put the block on the portal. This won't shut it down, only make it harder for anyone else to get through." She handed him a cloudy vial of inky liquid. "You know what this is for."

"Thank you. Let's pray it works." Rekkus gave his mate one more kiss before stepping back. "I love you, Dana. Myron, could you keep her at a safe distance?"

Rekkus stood in front of the opening doorway. "Cyrus, stop grinning like an idiot."

"Why are you grinning?" Shade wondered.

"Rekkus hates going into the city. The commotion his presence causes is amazingly entertaining."

"Do try and shut up, Cyrus," Rekkus growled. A flash of light signaled the portal ready, and, with a wink, he stepped through, followed by Cyrus.

"Tell your sister I'll be back tonight." Goddess, how Shade hated the portals. Stepping into darkness, he experienced the excruciating pull followed by unbearable tightening before the world brightened. When his eyes focused once more, he found Rekkus waiting, arms crossed, apparently unaffected by the portals. Perhaps it was a shifter thing.

But the man growled at the security guards—young shifters, and, from the smell of him, one of the tiger streak who had not the slightest idea who they were dealing with—and that was more of a Rekkus thing. "Do we intercede?"

"Oh hell, no." Cyrus slapped an arm across Shade's chest. "He can handle them."

"No one is scheduled to come through the Wiccan Haus portal for another three days," said one. Young shifters all had an overblown sense of self.

"We need some ID," insisted another.

"ID?" The dangerous softness to Rekkus' voice should have offered warning.

"Go on, Rek, show them your ID." Cyrus rubbed his palms together, grinning. "You didn't think you could get through the day without anyone knowing you were here, did you?"

Rekkus glared at him, and anyone other than his best friend would have cowered at the stare. An interesting dynamic there. Cyrus was being hunted by the worst the world had to offer and the villains were afraid of only Rekkus. The only person unafraid of Rekkus—with the exception of Dana—was Cyrus who worried about the assassins who were afraid of Rekkus. So the circle continued.

Before Shade could blink, Rekkus had his shirt off. "Why is he getting naked again?" Did this man do anything clothed?

Cyrus chuckled. "They asked for ID. This is the best ID Rekkus has."

Turning his back to the guards, Rekkus revealed the tribal tiger on his shoulder. A mere tattoo to the uninformed, but to paras it declared a prime. Rekkus had been born with it, as would one of the cubs.

"Highness." The tiger guard got to his knees, yanking the other one, a hawk shifter, down with him.

"Oh, for fuck sake. Get off the floor." Rekkus glared at the two. "Is there still a room between this door and the city?"

"Yes, sire."

"Don't sire me, and let us through. They are with me, so, unless you want me to rip off your heads, you will let us pass." Rekkus lingered as they moved past him. "And no one but us will go through this portal tonight. I expect you both will be here when we return at sundown."

"Of course, sire."

Inside the small entry room, Rekkus turned to face Cyrus. "Change your hair and eye color."

Chanting under his breath, Cyrus shook his head as if shaking powder from his scalp. The black color puffed out in a cloud, leaving a red rich tone. His eyes changed from their Rowan icy blue to a fierce orange.

"You look good as a ginger," Shade said to fill the silence.

"Is that what color it is?"

"He can change it but has no control over the result. You need to redo your eyes. You look possessed...much better." Rekkus handed him a vial he had taken from Sarka. "Now drink."

A testament of their friendship, Cyrus downed the inky liquid without questioning and with only a slight cringe. "What smells?"

"You." Rekkus walked out of the protective chamber. Since the security breaches, the only remaining portal to the island had been under strict watch.

"Me?" Cyrus sniffed the back of his arm then his underarm.

"The smell of your breath will make any para believe you are a shifter. Sage and Sarka have been working together on this for such an occasion."

"Rawr, cool." Cyrus strutted around, puffing his chest out. "So, what am I? Were wolf, bear, ooooh, dragon. Say I am a dragon."

Rekkus stopped, and Cyrus collided with his back. The tiger sniffed the air. "Otter."

"Otter? You can't be serious."

"Because I'm renowned for my witty repartee? Don't blame me. Talk to the Rowan ladies."

"What the fuck, Rekkus." Cyrus kicked a pebble. "How the hell am I supposed to get the ladies as an otter?"

Rekkus shrugged and kept moving, but Shade caught his smirk before he turned away.

They walked under an archway marked Portal Central. Once past it, the capital para city Lochmage would envelope them into its crazy hustle and bustle.

"Remove your gloves and put them in your pockets," Rekkus said, so low Shade barely made out the words.

Shade watched Cyrus remove the single protection he had from the visions which had nearly broken him six years before. Touching something could cause him to see everything the owner of that object had ever done. But Cyrus was so associated with those gloves, even with the change in smell and coloring they would be a dead giveaway.

"Cy."

"I will stay behind you and to your right at all

times. You will call me by my middle name should you need me, and I am to do everything you say without question. I am not to try and save you. I am to save myself blah, blah, and fucking blah. I know the drill."

Rekkus turned and lowered his voice. "I do not take any part of your safety as a joke."

"Neither do I, big guy." Cyrus leaned into Shade who had taken the stance to the left of Rekkus. "Sometime I feel I need a whip and stool to deal with him."

"I heard that."

"I hoped you had."

They walked the rest of the way in silence. Rekkus appeared to look straight ahead, not bothered by or interested in those around him, but they both knew he scanned. He listened and he was assessed. He had twelve escape routes already worked out. He did not, however, have any backup as they weren't giving any time to set it up.

Shade listened to the souls they passed. Some expressed concern and trepidation. Rekkus' temper was world renowned, as was his strength, but he also received respect for his even-handedness. They couldn't hide his presence in town, but, thus far, no one other than a teen girl, who thought Cyrus cute, had given the warlock a second look.

As long as the onlookers were filled with fear, curiosity, and, yes, a lot of lust all directed at Rekkus, Cyrus remained hidden in plain sight. The few hostile souls he sensed were young shifters wanting to show their skills, but they weren't stupid enough to think they could take on the tiger, although they would say they had to their friends later.

Turning down a dark alleyway, Rekkus knocked

on a large iron-riveted door. The watchman's hatch slid open with a loud clang of metal hitting metal. "State your name and business."

Rekkus growled from deep in the back of his throat, at the end of his patience.

Shade leaned against the wall. "He hates any social civility doesn't he, Cyrus?"

"It's gotten worse, the longer he stays at the Wiccan Haus. No one expects him to be anything but gruff, and he meets their expectations."

The hatch slammed shut as the big door slid open. "Dammit, Rekkus, is it too much for you simply to say Rekkus, it's Rekkus, instead of scaring the piss out of me?"

"Hamish." Rekkus gripped the other man's arm in greeting. "Lock the gate and make sure no one enters until I am gone. I want every single gate to remain closed."

"Yes, sire." The guard bowed and talked into a walkie-talkie while closing the gate behind them.

Rekkus didn't double-check. Hell, Shade doubted it ever crossed his mind his orders wouldn't be followed, especially by one of his kind. Though the guard had been of the golden streak, he would follow any commands given to him by this man. "You can put your gloves back on. In fact, I recommend doing so. We don't want to tempt the hags any more than we can."

They moved through the maze-like area until they reached the dark staircase. A few steps separated them from the open-air courtyard draped with the purple flowers of the weeping violet willow trees that lined the garden and offered ears to the ladies inside. The limbs moved to reveal the opening to the council's great hall. These trees, though beautiful, could be lethal, and no person could find the great hall without their allowing them to pass.

"As soon as we pass over the threshold, Cyrus, any illusions will disappear. But they should reappear as soon as you emerge again," Shade informed him.

"If it doesn't, one of the ancients will have to fix the issue. He can't leave different than he entered."

"And Sage's potion?"

Rekkus threw another vial at Cyrus. "You didn't think I would come ill-prepared."

Cyrus took on his usual self and Rekkus marched to the center of the dome-ceilinged room. He knew the drill, had been here often enough. First, as a young boy with his father. Later, as emissary of the Syndicate, and the last time as Cyrus' bodyguard after the murder of his own family. The man knew this room, these women, and what they expected. It didn't mean he had to like it.

He stood in the center of the room within the natural-lit circle. Perhaps not the Rowans, but most everyone else would show due respect to the three who governed all the para. Rekkus didn't. He stood before them flushed with anger, jaw gritted. His presence would be homage enough.

"Greetings, Prince." One of the three voices or perhaps all three, bounced off walls until it disappeared into the universe. From his position at the side of the room, Shade could not determine where they sat or who spoke.

"Why have you summoned me...now of all times?" Rekkus demanded.

"Why, indeed." Sarcasm would come from the vampire.

"How fares your wife?" Concern for a shifter's

cubs would come from another shifter.

"She lies unprotected and heavy with child while I play nice with you." He stood, arms crossed, feet apart in a stance declaring his obstinacy.

"We have very different definitions of nice, young Prince."

Clenching his fists at his sides, Rekkus said, "Do not call me meaningless titles."

A collective sigh washed over the room and the three men standing within. If they had hoped time had softened the beast there, they were mistaken. Not something they often admitted to. Shadedor's powers were useless in this room, much like Cyrus' charm, but it didn't take any magick to recognize they had hoped being mated had mellowed the tiger. Being wrong rarely sat well with the council. "It is meaningless because you refuse to add meaning to it."

"What is she talking about?" Cyrus whispered, tilting his head at just the right angle to keep his voice from traveling. Rekkus had trained him well.

"What does young Cyrus wish to know?" another voice asked. "Come into the light so we can see you better. Five years is but a blink in time to us, but for you it can be an eternity."

Cyrus hesitated. His life with the Syndicate had been hell. A talent he'd neither wanted nor could deny. His existence always in danger. Perhaps he didn't want to be in the presence of the three who had made his entire family a target of assassins. "Did you bring me here as a ruse, believing I would have him at my side?" Rekkus demanded.

"You forget who you talk to." At the rise in pitch of the collective voice, Shade and Cyrus covered their ears. Rekkus didn't flinch.

"I forget nothing," the tiger growled.

The air simmered with electricity. Few shifters could break the enchantments of the room to shift. Rekkus' father had been one of them, and rumor had it one of the elders bore scars to prove it. No one had a doubt Rekkus, whose powers had surpassed his father's by his teens, could do the very same.

"Sisters, there is no need for this hostility." Only the fae could calm a group so full of heated anger. "Rekkus, we brought you here as it is seven years to the day since we have last talked with you about taking your rightful place. The tigers are in need of their prime."

"And I am no one's king." His roar shook the walls.

"You are what the Fates have provided and you bear their mark to prove it."

"I have pledged my life to the protection of Cyrus. Nothing on this earth can break my blood bond."

"Nor are we asking you to. There is no reason you can't do your duties from the island. You would need to come to town but twice a year to deal with issues and disputes."

"The alphas of each streak can maintain their own, but there must be a prime. Many years have gone without one."

"Nine years have passed since my mother murdered the streak's prime." When he stepped forward, thirteen guards stepped from hiding to make their presence known.

Cyrus gripped his shoulder. "Rekkus, you will do no one, least of all Dana or I, any good locked in prison. Don't let them bait you."

"Cyrus, you seem to have lost your recklessness."

True. In times past, Cyrus and Rekkus would each have spurred the other on and laughed while the other got into trouble. Times and murders changed men.

"Perhaps, ladies"—Shade stepped forward feeling the tensions rise again—"we should let this issue pass at present. You have made your request, as was correct, at the seven-year mark. He must be allowed time to think on it and discuss it with his mate."

As Shade moved to the center of the room, his ability to tell which elder spoke increased. The vampiress's impatience matched that of Rekkus. "He has known his destiny since the mark appeared."

Shade placed a hand on Rekkus' other shoulder in silent warning. "The events leading to both men residing on the island have altered their desires. Rekkus, until the death of his father, was prepared to take his rightful place as prime in due order. We all knew that, but, like the council, he thought it would be years, if not decades."

"Years have passed." Silence reigned for a moment. "But you are correct. His mind is occupied with the upcoming birth of his cubs. We can table this for a bit, yet. But not forever."

"Can you assure us Cyrus' protection charms will return when he exits your door? His safety, as always, is everyone's concern," Shade asked.

"Of course."

"I'll consult with my mate, but there is one more thing," Rekkus said.

A hush came over the room.

Rekkus took a step in their direction. He must, like Shade, have honed in on their location. The thirteen guards tapped their spears on the ground in warning. "The portals," he growled. "I want them temporarily sealed when Dana goes into labor."

"How will we be informed when you unlock them?" Even they, with their great combined powers, couldn't see everything through the fog wall. Rekkus had ensured it.

"I will send someone through when they are to be closed. We will get a message to the same person who will, in turn, inform you."

Silence fell as Rekkus stood his ground. Most would have argued their case. Rekkus offered his explanation and subsided. He never sugarcoated anything.

"Do you have an idea of who will be sent through?" the shifter asked.

"Cemil. He could use a break, and the birth may overtax him," Cyrus said.

"Agreed. If you agree to have Shade remain on the island in his absence." A push from the fae to try and persuade hit them like a wave, but she hissed when it failed.

"Don't," Rekkus growled. The tiger could prevent such efforts—and she should not have tried.

"Shade stays on the island," the vampiress insisted.

Rekkus nodded then, before they could dismiss him, he grabbed Cyrus' arm and led him over the threshold. Shade stood back. He had his own business to discuss.

"This Dana?" the voice of the vampiress demanded. "What did you learn?"

"She carries three cubs. Two males and a female."

"Prime."

He braced himself. "Yes."

"Can she handle labor?" Concern laced the shifter elder's voice.

"She has no choice." In truth, he did not know if she could.

Silence again.

"And you, Shade? Where do you plan to take your mate when this is all done?"

He should have recognized they would be able to pick up on his life change. "She doesn't know yet, so I'm not sure. I'll inform you when I know."

"Leave us," the fae queen said. "We have other issues to deal with. But our minds are much at ease."

Shade found Cyrus and Rekkus at the far end of the commons, speaking with a guard. Cyrus, once again with copper locks, bore slight resemblance to his real self.

While Rekkus continued to speak with the other man, Cyrus approached Shade. "What did you tell them?"

"I assured them to follow Rekkus' instructions, the cubs were strong."

"And about my family."

"As I told you before, I am not on the island to report to them on you, only on the cubs, and that is all the information I gave them. I'm not their spy or your enemy."

"You understand my feeling toward those three lay high on the hostile scale." Rekkus tapped Cyrus' shoulder. "Let's get moving. The longer we stay in one place, the more we open ourselves up to someone discovering who you are."

As they walked out, Cyrus paused. "So, Shade, what exactly is going on with you and Ashlynn?"

***

Ashlynn woke at sunrise feeling as if her very breath had been ripped from her. Reaching for Shade produced air and a cold pillow. At five, the first time she woke, he had been there, awake and still stroking her back. She'd nuzzled into his side, feeling warm and protected.

Hours later, in the meditation room with her sister, the feeling, though less intense, hadn't vanished. Dana kept glancing at her grandmother's watch every two minutes. Ashlynn wondered why she always thought of Granny Mable as Dana's grandmother, not her own. Perhaps because Dana always went to visit her by herself. Granny never made Ashlynn feel less loved or left out, but neither did she invite her to spend the summer as she did Dana. Or had their mother refused in Ashlynn's name?

"What time do you expect them to return?" Ashlynn asked, trying to conceal her anxiety.

Dana peered out the window. "Sunset. For months, I wanted space. Now all I want is his arms wrapped around me. It's like...like someone ripped the air out of me. Sounds crazy, huh?"

She bit back her response, not wanting to play twenty questions with a sister who was looking for a distraction from missing her husband. But if Dana's feelings matched Ashlynn's and she was—how had she put it? Oh, yes, mated—what did that mean for Ashlynn? Hell, they had only met a few days ago, and she'd spent half of those thinking the man crazier than the craziest Looney Tune, though no less sexy.

They hadn't even had sex yet, something she planned to remedy as soon as he set foot on the island again. Maybe not so soon, as ravishing him in the hallway might raise an eyebrow or two, but soon after.

He had held her all night long, and, no matter how uncomfortable he must have been, never once had he acted anything but a gentleman. She had brushed against the proof of his sexual attraction to her several times. He'd smiled at her and helped her fall back to sleep. He did reposition himself a few times, but she pretended to be asleep to give him some relief.

So far, she and Dana had discussed her accident, her scarred face, and her disability. Dana asked questions no one else had thought to, like did she have a support system when she returned? Was there another kind of modeling she could do? Did she even like modeling? No one had ever asked her if she liked it or wanted to do it. They'd assumed she would.

She and Dana moved to safer conversations—gossip in the city, a few things Dana had heard about Frank, Dana's ex-fiancé, and his new lady, until they were left with the elephant in the room or, perhaps more to the point, the tiger. Ashlynn had to give her sister credit for dealing with everything so very well.

They had not talked about Shade, or about their mother, who did her very best to make every living soul who worked at the Wiccan Haus miserable. At least, today, she'd locked herself in her room and refused to come out, gracing the island with her absence. But she would emerge for dinner because the disgrace of being carried there bodily was too much for even her to stomach. Dana admitted Rekkus waited for the chance to "deal" with Mrs.

Stone.

"Deal with her?"

"I have to admit I was scared to ask," Dana said between sips of a shake Sage had brought to her. "Do you think they will notice if I wash this down the drain?"

"Don't you like it?"

"I can't get it down. I have no appetite. And if I don't finish it, they worry."

In the end, they snuck into one of the bathrooms together, breaking into a fit of giggles when another guest entered to find them standing over the toilet, watching the shake swirl down the drain. Running hand in hand, they took refuge in the library.

Their father stopped by sometime after lunch. Ashlynn wondered when he'd mention Dana's pregnancy, but she seemed okay with giving him time. They talked about the weather, the food, and about Ashlynn's head, which hurt more today than it had in days.

"Will you stay, Dad? And, Ash?" Dana asked. "Until the babies come?"

Her dad flinched, but Dana didn't comment on his response. He recovered and nodded. "I would love to."

"As would I." Ashlynn's mind wandered to the tall man with long hair like silk. Would Shade stay? Did it matter? It shocked her to discover it very much did matter. How could a man become so integral to her thinking in such a short time?

"I want you both there. It would mean the world to me, but I don't want Mother here. In fact, I want her gone as early as possible on Saturday. I can't have her hurting those who have been nothing but nice and caring to me. They accepted me, made me feel welcome. I won't have her being rude to those I love."

"No worries there. I'm surprised she hasn't started swimming already." Her father tucked a book under his arm.

"Perhaps we could recommend it." Ashlynn giggled.

He shrugged. "I'm off to find a quiet place in the apple orchard to read." His shoulders seemed bowed as he started off.

Dana smothered a yawn as she called good-bye to him.

"Are we boring you?" Ashlynn asked, keeping it light, but concern ran through her. It was enough to be pregnant, forget the fact she carried three babies. Add that those babies might be kittens some of the time and cold edges of panic covered Ashlynn.

Holy hell. She married a man who could change into a very large, rather scary-looking tiger. But the idea of him being a large cat did explain some of his personality traits.

"No, you aren't boring me." Another yawn. "But I do think I need to lie down for a bit. Housing these babies takes a lot out of me."

She scrambled to her feet to help the mama up. "Want me to walk you down to your place?"

"No. I promised Rekkus I would stay up here. The staff is on pins and needles as it is. Rekkus has a Murphy bed in his office." She let Ashlynn help her down the hall.

"Do tigers sleep in Murphy beds?"

"What?"

"Well, I tried to picture Rekkus pulling the bed down to sleep in it. Just seems like he would curl up in the corner or on a cat bed or something. Does he have one of those?"

Dana gaped at her.

"What?"

"No, he doesn't have a cat bed." Dana giggled before grabbing her belly to really laugh. She leaned against the wall until the glee subsided. Her face turning serious, she lowered her voice. "My understanding is, at one time, Cyrus didn't feel safe without Rekkus beside him. The only way for Rekkus to get any work done and ensure Cyrus could sleep was to install a bed where Rekkus could work."

Cyrus couldn't sleep without his bodyguard in the room? "Okay, so why does he need Rekkus?"

"You mean other than as his best friend? Because there are people whose only job is to hunt him down. Cyrus has powers I don't understand. Here we are." Dana indicated a small door marked Animal Control.

"Seriously?"

"Myron's idea of a joke. Rekkus says he doesn't give her any feedback good or bad; otherwise, she will get out of control." Dana punched in a code and turned on the light in the spacious office. "Can I get you to pull the bed down?"

"Of course." She followed her in, hoping to get some insight into her mysterious brother-in-law. She found an OCD's wet dream, the room immaculate, even the cork board organized. The only thing out of place was a black-and-white poster of a kitten with the words RAWR. I IZ A DANGEROUS TIGER. "Myron?"

"Got it in one."

After a second of fumbling with the cabinet door, she found the handle and pulled down the bed. "I like Myron."

"So do I." Dana eased onto the bed. "Can I be

silly? Would you go into the wardrobe? I am hoping there is a T-shirt balled up in the bottom of it."

Wasn't that so sweet it made Ashlynn want to gag? Sure enough, a T-shirt lay where Dana said it would be. She couldn't say her sister didn't know his habits, even if that one appeared out of place in the tidy office. She handed it over before shutting off the overhead light then slipped away. Her sister fell into a restless sleep before the door closed behind her.

"There you are." Her mother's voice wiped all semblance of relaxation away. "Is there some wild animal on the island you had to report?"

"What? Oh, yeah, something like that." She needed to move her mother away from the office door in case Dana woke. "Did you need me?"

"I haven't seen you today and thought we should sit down and chat."

Great. A chat with her mother always meant she would listen and agree with whatever her mother decided for her life. She didn't like the life she'd had before. She hadn't liked the person she had become.

She wasn't weak nor did she care a fig about the fame or prestige her mother so craved.

Her mother would no longer live vicariously through her. Squaring her shoulders, Ashlynn waved toward the front door.

"Fine. Shall we take a walk?"

"Getting far from this building suits me fine." Her mother headed toward the lobby at full pace—away from Dana.

As they passed Myron at the reception desk, and she paused. "Dana is resting...but you already knew, didn't you?"

"I did, but thank you for telling me all the same."

Myron smiled. "Good luck."

"Rawr?" She winked and mimicked a T. rex clawing the air.

"That's the spirit."

Her mother tapped her foot, the annoying I-will-not-be-kept-waiting attitude she always had. Ashlynn hurried because she didn't want to add to the argument they were sure to get into. "You seem to be rather chummy with the staff."

"I like them."

"You must be joking, Ashlynn. They, this whole place, is below you."

"No, Mother, they aren't." Ashlynn stopped, forcing her mother to do the same. "I never understood why a simple thank you or please was too much for you. Why you belittled and said hateful things when it wouldn't have cost you to be nice. And I never understood the way you behaved toward Dana. She did nothing but want you to love her, and you treated her worse than dirt on your shoe. She never acted up, she never argued, and yet she never could please you. Now she is about to make you a grandmother—"

"No, she isn't."

"She is pregnant and, though you disowned her, in a couple of weeks, maybe less, she will be bringing your grandchildren into this world." Leaving out the fact they were part tiger was the best decision. "Do you care so little, you aren't moved somewhat?"

"Moved to vomit."

This conversation was deteriorating at lightning speed. "How can you call yourself a mother?"

"I am not— Never mind."

Something hadn't been said, something the woman wanted to say but wouldn't or couldn't. A bad feeling passed over her, one of those premonitions you got when you knew things weren't right. Not in a "para" way, but in a trust your gut way. "What aren't you telling me?"

"It does not concern you."

"It does concern her." Dr. Stone appeared around the corner of the building. "And perhaps it's time we told the truth. This has gone on long enough."

"No, you promised." Her mother paled.

"Yes, and, as I told you two nights ago, I am also filing for divorce."

"I won't let you."

"You cannot stop me. I should've done it long ago, but I remained blind to what went on under my own roof."

"You didn't expect me to care for your bastard, did you? You had an affair, and I had to face the product of your infidelity every day and remember what you did."

"Wait, what?" Ashlynn blinked. The only muscles she seemed to be able to move were in her eyelids, so she blinked again and again. But, as the shock ebbed, it made a great deal of sense, and she realized this news would be welcome to Dana. Hell, maybe her mother would say Ashlynn spawned from another in a long line of her father's mistresses.

Her mother ignored her and tore into her father, threatening to take him for everything he had.

"Do you think I give a damn about money?" He raised his chin. "I've learned how to enjoy life again. Why do you think I fell in with Dana's real mother?"

"Because she would spread her legs to anyone."

"No, the sex came much later. She cared about

me, not my status. She cared about the man I wanted to become. A man I forgot existed. No more."

Decades of anger and frustration poured from them both. Vile things and then silence, as if they had run out of things to say. Words they had kept inside for so long left behind a great nothingness.

"Amazing how this happens." Ashlynn jumped, but Cemil's touch on her arm calmed even while the air sizzled.

"What do you mean?" Ashlynn couldn't look away from her parents.

"Why do you think you have been suffering from unexplained headaches?" He brushed her bangs from her forehead.

She jerked her attention from the parents she barely knew anymore to the blond man at her side. "Um, duh. I was knocked out by a lighting instrument."

"Yes, well, there is that. But I suspect it was building long before the accident, from the moment Dana took her leap of faith and broke from the family." Cemil pulled Ashlynn away. "It was the first time you realized you could escape, too, but your mother had her claws into you. Where she didn't love Dana, she did have some emotional connection to you. She saw her as a responsibility, a burden.

"But, deep inside, you knew something odd surrounded your house and a little voice warred with the person you had been trained to be."

"I still don't understand."

"We are victims of our environment. Even the gentlest of puppies can be turned into a killing machine under evil influences. You hid your light deep inside to protect yourself. And, I think, to protect your sister."

"Mother would hit her if I was kind." A memory hidden deep shot to the surface.

Cemil nodded as if the news didn't come as a surprise. "I believe that is information we should keep to ourselves. There would be no controlling Rekkus if the knowledge came to him."

"I've never spoke of it before. I didn't remember until now." She shook her head. A great weight lifted from her shoulders and head.

"Nothing can save your parents' marriage." Cemil stopped in the lobby.

"I don't think they should try."

"A healthy response to an unhealthy situation. But I am thinking it's you who needs to divorce them. Time to rebel."

Ashlynn watched the sun drop below the tree line. Her heart and other parts of her clenched. He would be here any moment. With a quiet shove from Cemil, she ran, stopping long enough to hear Myron say, "Synergy Room."

The Haus shook, followed by a loud rumble. Dana had said it happened every night, but Ashlynn hadn't believed her. At the end of the hall, two guards in black flanked the ever-formidable Sarka. "Only those three come through."

The guards nodded, and Cyrus, well, Cyrus with fiery hair, came into sight. A second later, Rekkus walked through then patted Cyrus down before nodding. Only then did Cyrus shake his head and the red disappeared. She stared at the swirling, inky cloud until Shade appeared. He leaned on the wall, gasping.

"I...hate...portals." His eyes met hers.

"Dana?" Rekkus asked.

"Sleeping in your office," Ashlynn replied.

Rekkus smiled and broke into a run down the hall toward his office.

She didn't think. She had spent too much time thinking, thinking about what was right. What everyone expected and what was normal. Now she needed to feel. Grabbing Shade's hand, she pulled him along until she found a door marked Synergy Room slightly ajar. Pushing it open, she towed him into the dark room. Ashlynn jerked off her sunglasses and, with a hand tangled in his hair, brought his lips down to hers, forcing his mouth open and tasting him with her tongue.

"What are you doing?" he asked when they paused, gasping for air.

"Rebelling."

"Oh, I like the sound of rebelling."

"You'll love how it feels more." Grinding her pelvis against his, she reveled in the moan escaping him.

"I'm not complaining" he whispered against her neck. "But what are you rebelling against?"

"My mother, and I don't want to think or talk about her anymore."

"I don't want to think about her either."

Holding her against the door, he worked down her body until he knelt before her. Anxious, she shimmied her pants into a puddle of expensive fabric at her ankles. He removed them, first one foot then the other, careful to keep her high-heeled shoes she wore secure on her feet. Another jolt of excitement ran through her as she watched his gaze follow the long line of her legs. She hadn't known why she put on heels today, seemed trivial and frivolous, but now she thanked heaven she had.

"I have never seen anything more beautiful." The truth lay in his expression for her to see.

"I want you."

He kissed her inner thigh, breathing deeply. "I know."

The lacy panties soon joined the pants leaving her bare from the waist down, with her blouse open but remaining on her shoulders for him to remove. The only article of clothing yet to be touched was the matching bra to her discarded panties.

Hooking her leg over his shoulder, he closed his eyes and drank from her like a man dying of thirst. She laced her fingers through his hair and with the other hand reached for anything to stabilize her. He wouldn't let her fall, but she sensed he would rock her world. In the end, her fingers closed around a towel rack.

She guided him, teaching him what pleased her and, in turn, she learned what pleased him as well. She could almost feel her fingers on his skin, as if he were touching her. As she tried to wrap her mind around little odd sensations, his tongue entered her and all thoughts vanished. He pressed her against the door, preventing her from moving. She might have started this, but he had taken charge.

Perhaps she had been celibate too long, but in the back of her brain a small voice she didn't want to listen to kept telling her the reason this felt so good, so right, had to do with the man as much as his technique. Behind her closed lids, an orange glow appeared.

Opening her eyes, she gasped. Sandstone rocks glowed, lighting the room. "Are those rocks humming?"

He pulled back, looked around, and smiled. "They are. I must not be as dusty at this as I had worried."

"How long has it been?"

"Longer than you care to know." Strong fingers gripped her hips, pulling her to meet his waiting mouth again. Thoughts of crystals left her mind as her stomach knotted, and she reached for him in time to have the first wave of inexpressible pleasure rack her. If she had been able to catch her breath, she might have screamed the building down, but she could no more whisper his name as yell it to the ceiling.

Relentless, his tongue worked her, and when she couldn't take another orgasm, the room spun. The pillows supported her as she lay horizontal below him. Clutching his shoulders, she lifted her head so she could kiss him again. Instinct overrode every thought as if her body no longer needed her brain to his lead in the dance. Her legs spread wide to make room for him. Her hips rose in welcome as his cock entered her in one quick, smooth stroke.

Gasping, she arched into him. Nails dug into his shoulders, begging for his body to move. He pounded into her like a stallion, speaking in a language she'd never heard before but somehow understood perfectly. Words of love, pleasure, and need. He told her in his own beautiful language, and showed her with his body, his desire both strong and pure.

She gave him all she had to give, offered him more. She would follow him to the end of the world. So when the orgasm enveloped her, she followed him over the edge and let the darkness take them both.

***

He had bound himself to her. Lying on the sea of pillows, he pulled her into his embrace. The crystals hummed as much from their passion as from his love.

"Can I ask you a question?" She ran fingernails over his flat stomach.

He took a stabilizing breath. "Anything."

"How did you get naked so fast? One second you were dressed, the next, boom, you were on top and naked. Is this some sort of Wiccan Haus magic?"

"No." He couldn't keep from laughing. "Quite the opposite. I think you would call it desperation, and I'm not naked. I hoped you wouldn't notice my pants hanging around my ankles. Not very sexy at all."

Reaching down, he pulled them up to prove his point then locked the door and helped her get dressed. Anyone could have walked in on them. He didn't want to share her with anyone, not this glow she had in the light. Reaching up, he caressed her scar. "You are so beautiful."

She pulled away as if the words burned her. "Maybe once, not now."

"Says who? Society? You are beautiful to me. Imperfectly beautiful, every inch." He let his lips brush over the jagged angry skin. "Perhaps one day you will see what I see in you."

"Will you be leaving tomorrow with the other guests?"

"No. I'll be here until the babies are born. Even without the babies I'd have stayed."

"Why?"

"Do you not know? Ashlynn, I'm in love with you. You are everything I want in a mate." Even barring the fact the Fates had already chosen her for him, he wanted her on a level not entirely having to do with his soul. She touched his heart as well.

"I couldn't stop thinking about you today," she murmured. "I felt as if a part of me had been ripped out. I don't understand, but it doesn't scare me as much as it did and I would like to give it a chance."

"Not to mention it would bother the hell out of your mother."

"There is that." Her smile fell. "Dana is my half-sister."

"And your mother plays the role of wicked stepmother."

"Yes."

"I suspected something of the sort. It didn't add up otherwise." It would be a relief to Rekkus that the woman wasn't kin, though, perhaps, it would be better for all around if he still had that as a leash. "How did Dana take it?"

"She doesn't know yet." The soft light reflected the pain in her hazel eyes. "Is it cowardly that I don't want to be the one to tell her?"

"Depends on what you are scared of."

"I don't want to be the cause of any more pain for Dana. I haven't always been the best sister. She needed me to support her after her botched wedding, and I did nothing but cower behind my mother, afraid to stand up for what was right."

"When you were little, what would happen if you and Dana played together?"

"Oh, there was no playing. I can't remember ever being in Dana's room or her in mine. Her room lay at the other end of the house. If I started toward it, my mother would snap at me."

"So, it's safe to say you were harshly discouraged from attaching yourself to your big sister in any way."

"Yes. Dana was forced to stand outside in the snow barefoot because I wore her shoes one day. My father didn't know about it, and no one dared go against my mother."

Shade tried to imagine a young Dana being punished in such a way, but his brain wouldn't allow it. "You were both abused by a callous woman. She played into your fears with venomous words and actions guaranteed to hurt."

Tears ran like two small rivers over her cheeks. "Dana wouldn't accept my apology the day of the shoe incident. She told me to shut up and stormed off. She never let my mother see her pain. One of the house staff snuck off to make sure Dana was okay, and mother fired her on some trumped-up charge the next day. But as much as I wanted to go make sure she was okay, Dana didn't want me to."

"Perhaps Dana wanted, no, needed, to protect you as well. She might have felt the only way to do that was for her to prevent the natural relationship from forming." With the pad of his thumb, he wiped away her tears. "Do you want me to ask one of the siblings to break the news to Dana? I think she will be relieved."

"I would be." But she nodded.

"Done, but I think we should do it after your mother is on the ferry back to the mainland." He pulled her close. "The siblings will know best when to break the news.

After allowing himself the luxury of holding her in his arms for a little while longer, he got up and helped her to her feet. Myron would keep anyone out of the room, and he doubted after her little greeting at the portal Sarka would send security after either of them. But they needed to get some food because he didn't plan on making this a one off.

She had awakened a sexual appetite he planned on feeding until he was satisfied. In the back of his mind, the niggling worry this feeling would disappear as it had with his parents arose. But, unlike his Shenshaw mother who understood the process of bonding, Ashlynn would think she hadn't been good enough. Lifting his eyes to the heavens, he closed them and prayed the Fates would be kind. If this feeling left him, he wouldn't be aware if she was in pain, because once an ability to read a soul had been taken, it didn't return.

When the full moon crested over the sea, his future and hers would be sealed.

Chapter Nine

"Perhaps you and your father can focus on your healing," Sage said as they stood on the hill, watching the ferry pass from sight. She placed her hand into Ashlynn's and held tight.

"I'm glad Dana decided not to see her off." Ashlynn had expected her to be there to say good-bye—closure she called it. Dana took the news of her maternal heritage well, the Rowans reported. But everyone—including Ashlynn—agreed Rekkus should be told after Mrs. Stone stepped off the ferry on the mainland.

"I have a feeling it wasn't her decision to miss it. Rekkus was pretty adamant that nothing good could come from her being there." Sage turned back toward the Haus. "But perhaps there wouldn't be closure either way."

"With my mother, probably not. So, did Dana tell Rekkus?"

Sage gave an unladylike snort. "If he knew, I am not sure your mother would have made it off the island in one piece. Where is Shade?"

Ashlynn shrugged. Everyone here seemed to know everything everyone did. "He left before I woke." She rubbed her temples, another headache forming, but less intense than usual.

"Do you need a shake?"

"I don't think so. I've been stressed about this morning. Worried Mother would insist I come with her. But, in the end, she got on the boat with not so much as a good-bye. Good thing I don't have anything important still at my parents' house. It would be in the trash by the time I got home."

"We allowed your father to use the office phone to call his lawyer and his work. Perhaps you need to contact the attorney as well. You sure there is nothing there you'd like someone to fetch for you?"

"No. Nothing special. And she'll be too busy badmouthing my father. If she spoke ill of her poor, injured daughter, she would only come across as a bad mother. To her, image is everything." And above all, she could be thankful for small things. She had nothing to lose. She had no job, no real friends, and her relationship remained here. She had become closer to her sister than she had ever imagined. "Not that I care what she says to her shallow friends."

The Haus stood strong in the mist of chaos. She had been warned it would be this way as they prepared for the new week. They had a couple of hours from when the ferry left with the humans and returned with the new guests. The paras left at sunrise and the new arrivals would show up at sunset. But, this sunset Cemil would leave through the portal. They needed someone they trusted on the other side to close the portals and ensure they stayed closed until after Dana delivered. Sending Cemil also ensured the empath wouldn't be overwhelmed by

Dana's pain. His presence on the other side also served to reassure the Syndicate the Rowans were not using the situation as a trick to close the island from all future interference.

Shade had agreed to take over Cemil's classes for the upcoming week, and all the paras coming through were warned they might not get back in a week, as the portals would be going through maintenance.

"What kind of maintenance would the portal require?" Ashlynn asked.

"I haven't the foggiest idea, but, then, neither does anyone else, so it plays to our advantage. The longer the portal stays down, the louder chatter in the capital will become. For everyone's sake, the sooner Dana births these babies the better."

"Will Cemil be in danger?"

"Rekkus has some men in the city he trusts to take care of Cemil. And, much like Cyrus, he will disguise his appearance. He is much stronger than he looks and can take care of himself."

It seemed Rekkus knew everyone and had connections everywhere. Shade's staying remained her main concern. He sidestepped any conversation about the future, saying they would have to see what happened. But she had never felt closer or more in touch with a man than she did with him in the bedroom.

"Can I ask you something?"

Sage cocked her head. "Of course."

"How old is Shade?"

"Why not ask Shade?"

"I did and all he would say is 'I am older than you can imagine.' Which...."

"Makes you more curious. Honestly. I don't

know how old he is." She closed her eyes and tapped her foot. "Wait, he is at least.... Perhaps you should sit down for this."

Ashlynn asked no questions because every time someone on this island said sit down she either wished she had or was glad she listened. Taking a seat in one of the overstuffed leather armchairs of the Haus, she nodded, ready to hear whatever Sage had to say.

"As I said, I am not sure of his exact age. He was born sometime after the American Revolution and before the Civil war."

"Making him over a hundred years old."

"Closer to two hundred is my thinking."

She leaned forward in the chair and thought she might start hyperventilating. "Years. You...are...talking...years."

"Can someone get me some water, please?" Sage turned to a small, older woman who was arranging flowers across the room. "Perhaps I should have broken it easier."

Ashlynn asked, "How?"

"No idea." Sage touched her back, making calming circles.

"What happened?" She couldn't bring herself to look at him. Not yet. What was age? Except he happened to be older than her great-great-great-grandfather. And as she aged, he wouldn't.

His face. Not a single line or whisker marred his face. "Two hundred years old?"

"Dammit, Sage. She wasn't ready."

"When would she be ready?"

"Not here in the lobby."

"Don't you dare yell at her," Ashlynn demanded. "She at least answered my question."

Crouching, he cupped her face in his hands. "I didn't know how to break it to you, but I had planned to do it this week. On my time."

"Well, your time sucks."

Shade cursed, picked her up, and carried her off. She fought for a second but didn't want to around a lot of people anyway and didn't think her legs could carry her.

"Push the fucking button," he bit out.

He was mad, no, furious. Reaching out, she did as he demanded. Otherwise, they would be standing here forever as the elevator to her floor wouldn't work for him. She laid her head on his shoulder and held her peace until they were ensconced within the privacy of her room. He lowered her with great gentleness onto the bed.

"How can you be over a century old?"

"My people are called Shenshaw. We are ancient, dating from the Middle Kingdom of Egypt, maybe before. We aren't immortal, but we live a very long time."

"There is more, isn't there? I've sensed it since the other night when we first made love. You pull away as if you are afraid of hurting me."

"There is something else." Walking to the windows, he closed the drapes before lowering the lights then returned to her side. He lifted her from the bed and carried her to the large, comfortable chair. She adjusted herself on his lap so she could see him. He removed her glasses and looked into her eyes. "I love you. I have told you numerous times, and I know you feel the power of my feelings for you. You overwhelm me."

She cupped his cheek and placed her lips against

his forehead. "I love you, too."

As the words washed over him, his head went back, and he breathed deep. She hadn't said them to him before. She had felt the emotion, but, until now, hadn't understood the need to say and to hear them. She knew he struggled with words to tell her something, but what could be harder to tell her than he happened to be a century and half old? But she always felt secure in his love.

"My people don't feel strong emotions. Sex is a physical release but not emotional."

"That's awful."

"Yes and no. Can you imagine how hard it would be to do my job if I had Cemil's empathy? The depression my kind would endure would be overwhelming. The goddess knew and understood we could only take so much. She wasn't without sympathy, though. Every once in a while we find someone who gives us emotions. Lets us feel."

"And that's me for you." Elation wrapped her.

"It is." He didn't appear overjoyed. "But I only feel it for you. I will be happy when meeting the new babies. I am saddened by the loss of a friend. But I can only feel strong emotions when associated with or around you."

If it was a good thing, why did he refuse to meet her gaze, and when she went to touch his cheek pull away? "There is a but coming."

He leaned back in the chair. "There is. If the person who gives us the emotion isn't our soul mate, our true soul mate, we lose the emotion after the first full moon passes."

"Meaning?" She dreaded hearing what it meant, but they needed it on the table. Better she know than worry.

"Meaning, when the moon crests tomorrow night, I will either be still madly in love with you or feel nothing again." He reached out and ran a finger down her scar. "I don't care about me. It's you I worry about. You are human; the moon will have no effect on how you feel."

"So, tomorrow night, I will either be loved or heartbroken."

"Yes."

"Well." She laid her head on his shoulder. "Let's not waste any more time. If I only get your love for another day, then I don't want to talk about losing it. I want to feel your love."

He held her close, and, for a moment, she let herself believe they would get lucky. She asked him about his life, discovered he was in fact one hundred and sixty eight years old and, to his people, he hadn't even entered middle age. They both had been devoid of feelings until they met each other. It made the idea of losing him so much harder to deal with.

"Don't think about it."

"I thought you couldn't read me." She reached for a hot, crusty roll. Jarred from their embrace by a knock on the door, they'd opened it to find Sage holding a tray of delicious food and the news they were excused from the dining room for the evening. Myron had convinced her to make the exception.

"I can't read you, but it doesn't take para power to make an educated guess. Come on, let's head to bed."

They undressed each other, anticipation building, but, in the end, they held each other tight. She needed to feel a closeness to him which had nothing to do with sex.

***

"She's in labor and she hasn't told anyone yet," Myron said as soon as they came out of the elevators. "And, no, Rekkus doesn't know or he wouldn't be off with the teens on the training field."

"Why haven't you told him?" Ashlynn asked, wondering why Myron would be telling them first.

"'Cause I promised I wouldn't read Dana anymore, or him, for that matter." She held up the cards in defense. "And I wasn't reading her, I swear, but the vibe became so strong the cards told me what needed to be shared. I can't always control what they tell me. I hoped perhaps you could go down and confirm she is in labor and send up the alert."

Shade eased the cards from Myron and, with care, left them on the desk. "Stop fretting. Your cards will tell you no more than they have. Ashlynn will go down because a sister going to visit is normal and no one would think anything of it."

Myron had the good grace to blush. "I'm using you to avoid getting into trouble with the great big puss in combat boots, but...."

"No worries but...can you maybe answer a question for us?" Ashlynn asked, chewing on her cuticle. Maybe Myron already knew if they would remain soul mates in the morning.

"She can't," Shade said, and her hopes fell. "I already asked her."

"I guess we should head down to the cabin and find out how fares my dear sister, then."

When they reached the lagoon, they could hear labored breathing and moans coming from inside the cabin. Bursting inside, they found Dana doubled over, holding her side, grasping the countertop so hard her knuckles were white. "Dana."

"Ash." Tears filled her eyes.

Ashlynn rushed to her side. "Shade, go get...everyone." She'd expected to find Dana in early labor, the type she had heard her father talk about when on call. The go bake some cookies and phone again when the contractions are closer together kind of labor. Dana had reached the meet me at the hospital phase. No wonder Myron's cards were reading what was going on. "How long have you been in labor?"

"Since last night." She took a big cleansing breath and straightened, breathing out a sigh. "I didn't want anyone to fuss."

"Well, prepare yourself. The fuss is on its way, and I expect your husband is going to freak."

As if on cue, the door flew open and the black tiger filled the doorway, his immense chest heaving. Ashlynn had no clue how far the training fields were, but they couldn't be close and, even if Shade had the guards at the top of the hill call Rekkus, it took him a minute or two tops to arrive. The tiger continued to stare, but, when Dana squeaked in pain, he shifted and strode to her side.

And, as nice as his ass might be, having her sister's mate standing so close to her naked was still disconcerting. "Get. Dressed."

"I will when this contraction is over. Relax. Remember what Trixie said."

"Fuck Trixie and get dressed," Dana barked.

"I got her. You go get some pants on." When he didn't move, Ashlynn stared him down. "She is never going to relax with me here and you naked, and in about three minutes there are going to be a hell of a lot more people here. This is about her needs, not yours."

"Sorry, you're right. Be back."

Once he was out of the room. Dana exhaled. "Nicely done, but did he just walk into the pantry instead of the bedroom?"

"I didn't want to say anything but, yes, yes he did." She fought a giggle, but when Dana laughed, she grinned. "I guess he's a little overwhelmed."

Dana paced around the room, Ashlynn at her heels.

"Do you want to sit?"

"No, walking helps. Perhaps outside." Dana made her way out of the cabin, stopping when another contraction hit. Rekkus came running outside, apparently having found the bedroom. He clutched one of her shirts in his hand. He stared at the flowered blouse and threw it to the side. He'd tried—even if he didn't realize he'd grabbed the wrong shirt until he'd almost tried to put it on. Not completely dressed, but at least the man had pants on. And his chest came a close second to being as nice as his ass. Not as nice as Shade's, in her opinion, but enjoyable nonetheless. And she wouldn't demand he cover up. She might love Shade, but it didn't mean she couldn't still appreciate fine art.

Of course, Shade chose the very moment to arrive. "Myron says we have hours yet. Sage is getting some things together and will be down in a few minutes."

Running full speed, Cyrus stopped before Dana and doubled over, attempting to catch his breath. He raised a finger. "Give me...a second."

"By the goddess, Cyrus." Rekkus threw a bottle of water at him from the cooler outside the cabin. "Did you run all the way from the training field?"

"You...bat...hell."

Which she interpreted as, You ran like a bat out of hell.

Rekkus eyed him. "Yes, but I'm her mate. It's not like we were under attack."

"Didn't...know...." He threw the empty water jug at Rekkus before finding a seat and dropping into it.

The next few hours flew by in a mix of contractions lasting forever and time flying by while standing still all at the same time. Stupid, but no one would leave. Dana seemed to have found her inner focus which included watching her husband but not hearing him. She insisted his voice made her want to do ultimate bodily harm to him. Yet if he moved out of sight, stopped touching her, she burst into tears.

"Hormones are a crazy thing," Sage said when she had been down to make sure Dana ate. With Shade's help, she checked on the welfare of the cubs. Dana's dad accompanied Sage at each visit but stayed in the background, prepared to assist if needed but informing them Sage had control.

What did her dad know about delivering paranormal babies?

"This wasn't how I imagined spending today," Ashlynn said, laying her head on Shade's shoulder as they watched Rekkus support his wife, from a distance. Serena had been pacing her cottage porch for the last hour, biting her fingernails in worry. Even her husband hadn't been able to calm her. "She is going to chew her thumbnail down to the cuticle."

"She can't deal with a woman in trouble or pain."

His fingers in her hair forced a sigh from her. "It doesn't matter how I spend today, as long as I can feel."

They hadn't talked about the soon-to-be setting sun, or the ticking time bomb that stood between them. She loved the simple ability to rest her head on his shoulder and touch him as she wanted. Her stomach clenched at the thought he might pretend nothing changed to prevent from hurting her.

Shade stood up and broke into a run seconds before Dana gripped her belly and threw her head back with a quiet scream to the sky. She panted and sweat broke out on her skin. "They're shifting. The males are scared."

Rekkus turned to Shade then to Cyrus. "Prepare the surgical theater."

"No!" Dana begged.

"We are getting it ready." Sage stayed calm and in control. "We don't have to use it."

"Let me help." Serena came over. "I know I can."

Ashlynn, who stood a few feet away, could only imagine how the sweet yet naive blonde planned to help. But she intended to find out. Besides, she had no doubt in about ten minutes Rekkus would carry Dana into the OR. She watched Rekkus and Serena argue over her "helping." In the end, Shade spoke up for the other lady.

"She might be the best person to help. We should try. Rekkus, we don't know how the cubs will react to the anesthesia. They could shift immediately."

The number one fear, the babies shifting into their animal state now loomed before them. If Dana had been born a shifter, it wouldn't be an issue. Her uterus would have been designed to deal with teeth and claws. But, if they shifted, they could tear her human uterus apart from the inside. And, if they sedated her, it could kill the cubs. In Ashlynn's mind, it would have been safer for them to have adopted.

"Rekkus." Serena laid a hand on his arm. "I can do this. I can help."

"Fine."

"You have to release me. You have to say it."

"I release you from your contract."

Serena let her hair down and walked to the water. It seemed to come alive around her. "Bring her in. Wherever is comfortable."

Rekkus lifted her into his arms and waded until he stood waist-deep. Serena who, oddly enough, remained fully dressed moved deeper before diving in. A second later, she crested with a tail. A bright shimmery tail of fins.

"Did she...? Holy hell."

"She's amazing, isn't she?" Kaleb arrived at Ashlynn's side. "If Rekkus has released her to sing, then things can't be going well."

"They aren't."

"My money is on Serena. Come on." He led her to the water's edge where she could see and hear better.

Serena rubbed Dana's belly, closed her eyes, and smiled. She asked Rekkus to let Dana stand on her own and turned to the other men on the shore. "Cyrus, are you ready?"

"Wh-what did you say? I can't hear you. I have earplugs in." Cyrus' voice echoed through the cove.

"Shade, you might want a pair," Kaleb said.

"No, I won't need them."

"What are the earplugs for?" she asked.

"Serena's talents lie in bending men's souls to

154

her will. The only ones she can't are those who are gay, or have found their soul mates. In those cases, their souls aren't interested in what she has to offer."

"While she is singing, I'm going to get something to eat," Cyrus yelled before heading into Rekkus' cabin.

"Probably wise. He gets louder and louder." Kaleb smiled at his wife, the love obvious to anyone who cared to pay attention.

Serena made light patterns through the water on Dana's belly. "Relax, my friend. You are safe. I won't let anything happen to you. Lean into Rekkus and let him support you. Ah, there you are, my little tigers."

Come, babes soon here,
Your time draws near.
Your mother grows weary
We know you are leery
Embrace the love around.
Come now it's time to come down.

"Don't stop, Serena. It's working." Shade waded out to join them and placed Rekkus' hand upon the extended belly. "Rekkus, your daughter is scared now. She doesn't understand why her brothers are suddenly so docile. You must talk to her. You must reach out to her. She needs her alpha."

Rekkus spoke in another language Ashlynn thought might be Gaelic. Dana laid her head back resting it on Rekkus' chest as the sun shone on her face. Ashlynn would have given anything to have a photographer present. Her sister had never been more beautiful, more at peace, or more powerful.

Contractions came and went with Dana cradled in Rekkus' loving arms. Her sister and brother-in-law worked as a team. He rubbed her head and spoke to her of love and admiration, stroking her damp hair from her face. Time seemed to both stand still and move at the speed of light.

Shade, Ashlynn, and Kaleb, sitting in the sand, still watching and listening, were joined by Sage and Dr. Stone. "Myron said it's time to get her into the house. The moon is rising. Let's hope these babies are more agreeable than their da."

Sage soaked the bottom of her skirt, approaching the trio as she entered the shallows of the lagoon. "Serena, how long will your song affect them?"

"It's hard to tell. They are so little but they're strong willed like their parents. I can assure twenty minutes, but not much more."

"Go rest and get something to drink, but we might need you again."

She nodded. Kaleb jumped to his feet to assist his wife out of the water.

Shade informed Ashlynn, "She has never sung so long. I also suspect there might be a slew of men in the vicinity who have all been lulled to sleep. Shame her song doesn't work on everyone. It might be a better means of having people sleep through the portal opening."

"Come on, Dana. Let's see if you can't walk into the cottage. Unless you have changed your mind and wish to deliver here?"

Dana shook her head and took three steps before Rekkus lifted her high into his arms.

"Rekkus, I said for her to try and walk. It's good for her to—"

"Sage, I have her."

Sage glanced at the sky. "Give me strength as I deal with protective men."

Despite his overprotectiveness and surliness, he

alone inherently knew what she needed. Ashlynn had been surprised to see her sister so peaceful, almost as if asleep in his arms as they passed. Sage and two other women Ashlynn had never seen before followed him into the cottage. The doors and windows closed behind them as if by...magic.

Cyrus came out a second later, pulling his earplugs out. "All right, Sage," he called over his shoulder. "No need to be bossy."

"So now we wait." Shade settled on one of the Adirondack chairs near the house. "I need to stay close to read their souls in case Serena needs to come back, but you are welcome to take a walk if you need to, Ash."

"No, I want to stay. With you." She climbed into his lap, laying her head on his shoulder.

"I am betting the Haus is an understaffed place right now. Poor Myron is forced to hold down the fort tonight."

"Why?" She loved the way his voice rumbled in his chest against hers.

"Sarka will have pulled twelve other witches for the coven's protection circle. On a good day, there are fourteen of us on the island. One extra in case of emergency. Sage is down here, as obvious am I. Cemil is off island, so she will have pulled two from our guests. Not ideal, but I'm sure worth it for the bragging rights. Not many are invited into Sarka's circle, and to protect Rekkus' babes, you can imagine. But that means there are fewer staff in the kitchen and for classes." Cyrus focused up the hill in the direction of the Haus. "Sarka sent word this afternoon to Cemil, letting him know Dana's labor had begun, so he is close to the portals in case he needs to reopen them to return."

"Wouldn't it be safer to keep them closed until morning?"

"Word will travel and get out. Reopening the portals can be dangerous. Best to have it done when no one is ready."

From then, no one spoke. Shade listened to the souls in a bit of a trace as he held tight to Ashlynn. Cyrus paced, pausing from time to time to stare at the cottage. Her father stood near the water, smoking a cigar, a bad habit he had promised to quit after the babies were born. But he stayed close in case his daughter needed him. Serena returned and entered the house as her husband jogged up the hill, to lock down the barracks, he said.

Ashlynn listened for high-pitched sound of a newborn's first cries, praying for something to prevent the full moon from cresting. She wished she could be in the room with her sister, helping in whatever way was possible, but she knew there was simply no room in their small bedroom for one more person who would just be in the way. "Will Rekkus change into the tiger when the moon rises?"

Cyrus paused. "No, he becomes more powerful during a full moon, but it doesn't force a shift. Teenage shifters can't regulate it. Their hormones are out of whack as is the problem with newborn and unborn babies. Rekkus will teach them to control it. Usually at about two they can get a handle on the need. And then all hell will break loose again around thirteen."

"So the teenagers I keep seeing are shifters."

"Yep, and some have been coming here every month for years. Rekkus is kind of an uncle to the boys."

A scream erupted from the cottage followed by a long deep grunt, both from Dana.

All became eerily quiet. As if no one occupied the cottage. Then the door opened and Serena walked out with a swaddled bundle. Smiling, she handed the baby to Cyrus. "There aren't enough idle arms inside. Rekkus insisted I give him to you. Meet Rhys Cyrus Duteigr."

"They named him after me?" Cyrus asked, his eyes glistening.

"Who else would they have named him after?" Serena asked as if it were the only choice they had.

Cyrus reached for the baby then hesitated. "Has anyone touched the blanket?"

Serena shook her head and showed him her gloved hands one at a time. "No one. Trixie even wore gloves when she knitted them."

He yanked at his black gloves with his teeth and threw them to the ground. Careful of the newborn neck and head, Cyrus lifted him from Serena and tears filled his eyes. She scanned his hands for scars or disfigurement but they were perfect and, to all appearances, normal.

Serena went back into the house, first dropping a kiss on the small baby's head, Ashlynn approached and, as she would have touched the child or the blanket to see better, Shade tugged her back against his chest. He whispered into her ear. "The reason Cyrus wears gloves is he can see the lives of those who have touched items. If he were to touch something you own, he would see and live your pain, your trauma."

"All of it, even from a second's contact?"

"Perhaps not all, not from fabric, but whatever experiences are strongest. Those tend to be painful experiences, not the gentle happy ones." Shade rubbed her shoulder. "This is heaven for him. This is peace. Because as each of these babies takes their first breath, all memories of past lives leave them. They are clean slates."

Ashlynn watched the euphoria covering Cyrus' handsome face as he held the child close. She turned to see the first edges of the moon over the water. She'd always loved the moon, but not tonight. Tonight, she wished it away, never to return. Two babies still need to be birthed, and Shade had told her that the biggest danger was that the babies would shift under the full moon. They wouldn't be able to help it and it could kill Dana. As if that wasn't enough, she didn't think she could deal with the loss of Shade.

A moment later, Serena came outside and, without ceremony, placed the baby into Ashlynn's arms. "Shade and Dr. Stone, Sage needs you both. I cannot help the girl child."

Serena led them into the house, leaving Cyrus and Ashlynn holding two precious babies and staring at the door. "She'll be fine, right?"

"Rekkus won't let anything happen to Dana. You can count on it." But uncertainty crossed his face. "Rekkus cannot live without her. She is too important to him. She is his reason for everything. And, yet, he has told her over and over she is free to leave. He wouldn't stop her if she were to get on the boat. If that isn't true love, I don't know what is."

Ashlynn's heart seized, and she turned in horror to see the moon as large as she had ever seen it hovering like a large orange ball above the water. She prayed for it to disappear. After the initial jolt, she didn't feel any different but, then, Shade had said it would be him who wouldn't feel anymore.

"You must trust what the Fates have planned," Cyrus said. "If Shade is the one, nothing will have changed when the moon rose."

A feminine growl full of frustration, exhaustion, and power erupted inside the house. The lights flickered on the porch followed by an eerie silence. And then, as the moon rose over the horizon, the sound of another baby's cry. This one tired but no less powerful. A lump formed in the depths of her throat, and tears rolled from behind her glasses. She laughed as she cried and did the only thing she could do while she waited. She held her nephew tight and told him how blessed he was.

***

Dana might be weak and tired, but her soul is strong. Shade stood across the room to assess. It had been touch and go when the third baby turned transverse breach and Sage attempted to turn her. Serena had been able to keep the boys calm during the delivery but had no power over the girl who portrayed a strong stubbornness and didn't want to be born yet.

Moreover, the little one knew when she took her first breath she would forget. She wanted to remember why she had chosen to come back. With Dr. Stone and Shade telling Rekkus the right things to say, they turned the baby. And as Shade sensed the moon crest, he watched the baby gaze up at her father with large blue eyes, inhale, and simply forget. At the same moment, he watched a father fall in love with his daughter.

And he, Shade, experienced the joy and the peace of a soul healing.

The moon had crested, and he felt.

He wanted to run out and wrap his arms around Ashlynn and bask in the feelings growing stronger, but Sage still needed him, and he had to take care of Dana, exhausted and not yet done with labor. She bled, and Shade remained silent on the matter. Sage and Dr. Stone were calm. He would deal with the tiger prime who was anything but. With his little girl in his arms, legs apart in protective stance, he watched, his queen lie helpless in the bed.

Tonight, she had earned the title, whether he informed her or not, but something else had happened. Something no one, not he nor Myron, had seen coming. The birth of her daughter had unlocked powers she'd hidden and buried. Powers passed down from a grandmother much loved. What powers and how strong would remain to be seen.

Minutes seemed like hours until Dana's color returned to normal and she demanded to see her babies. In that moment, she retook control of her life. Shade could leave, his job done. Sage waved him toward the door and followed him out.

"Dana would like to see her babies. Would you both like to come in and see her briefly? Then we need to leave the family alone," Sage announced.

Ashlynn walked by him with the second baby, Brynn Cemil, in her arms. Fear dimmed her eyes, even behind the glasses. He reached for her with his whole being, brushed her cheek, and smiled. "I still love you."

"Oh my." She grazed his lips with hers and

stepped into the very crowded bedroom. Kissing the baby, she handed him over to his mother. "I love you, Dana, but I have to go."

"Okay," she said, but her focus remained on the dark curly head of her second son.

"He loves me."

"Of course he does." She touched the downy hair then blinked at them both. "He is your soul's mate."

"How can you tell?" Ashlynn inched toward the door.

Dana shrugged as her attention shifted to her husband.

Ashlynn didn't wait for Dana or anyone else to speak. She ran from the room into Shade's waiting arms. He kissed her in the living space of her sister's house in view of the bedroom and the full moon. "Be mine."

"Always."

"Always could be a long time."

"For you. You're ancient."

Leading her from the house, he steered her to the water's edge. "If you accept me as your soul mate, you will live and one day die with me. You don't have to decide now. You have until the next full moon."

Pushing her hair behind her ears, she asked, "I can't decide now under this one?"

"No, it's a decision to be thought on and not made in the heat of passion. But we have a month to learn and feel. For you to heal and for me to adjust to new feelings."

"Sounds like we have a lot to do."

"Perhaps we can have a wedding and reception here, on the island, under the full moon as well as our own private soul mate acceptance."

Tilting her head, she asked, "Are you asking me

to marry you, Shadedor."

"Not very romantic. Sorry."

"I think it is the most romantic proposal I could ever want and I can think of no other place I would rather be wed than here with my sister and her family. Will they let my dad come back?"

"Providing your mother doesn't, I believe so."

She stopped in her tracks. "I don't think my mother will have much to do with us anyway."

"Are you all right with not seeing her again?" The inability to read her soul and her emotions would take some getting used to.

"I will get there. It's not what I had hoped, but...." She shrugged. "She's never been the mother I would have hoped for."

He didn't say anything in response because nothing he could say would ease her pain or help her to reconcile her new life. He held her and walked her up to the Haus. They almost collided with Cemil hurrying in the other direction. He waved but didn't stop, no doubt anxious to meet the newest members of the island because this place was a family. Not by blood but by choice, which made it so much more special.

"I do a lot of traveling," Shade said. "Will you join me?"

"I love to travel, but, at the moment, I would love to feel your arms around me and my legs wrapped around you. Naked, definitely, we should be naked."

"Naked is always good."

They waved at Myron who yelled out her congratulations to them both.

"Don't read us," Shade said with a smile.

"I didn't, it doesn't take a card reader to see true

love and it's written all over both of you." Myron went back to her cards but paused. "Dana?"

He knew what she read in her card—a new beginning for Dana, but it didn't refer to the babies or her new title. "She will need time to adjust and discover. Allow it to happen naturally."

"What naturally?" Ashlynn asked, pushing the elevator button.

"I believe the birth of your niece unlocked a para element hidden deep in your sister."

The doors opened, and she inhaled as she pressed the three. "My mother used to call her grandmother a witch, I always thought she merely insulted her."

"Perhaps, perhaps not. But Dana has taken enough of my thoughts. Tonight, I would rather think of you." Shade looked down at Ashlynn, his desires echoed back at him. He had to get her up to her room before getting her naked. In the end, they left a trail of clothes but managed to get to the bed in the nick of time.

Epilogue

Chaos. No other word described the amount of people who had been through the small cabin doors. He suspected another addition to the cabin would be on the horizon. Cemil, who appeared refreshed and at peace, moved from babe to babe unable to get enough of any of them. Sarka made an appearance making the right sounds of oohs and ahhs, but her blessing of protection had been heartfelt and strong. Sage, exhausted from the birth, had been the first to leave when the members of Rekkus' team came in to meet the newest island's inhabitants. And everyone from the kitchen staff to the cleaning crews wanted to see the babies.

Three perfect babies, each with ten fingers and ten toes. The boys, both dark haired and golden eyed fussed when one of them was too far from their sister. They seemed to be connected and, like their daddy, had a protective streak a mile wide. Neither had shown the sign of who would be the alpha and who the prime. Time would tell. Kalina, much like her namesake, remained quiet. Her white-blonde hair led Cyrus to believe when she shifted she would resemble her deceased aunt, a white tiger.

Myron had been the last to come down. She needed to wait until the babies had been bathed to appease her Romney traditions. Pulling a glass bottle from her bag, she asked, "May I?"

Rekkus nodded and Dana looked confused. "She wants to place some oil on the babies?"

Dana's brow furrowed.

"I only wish to strengthen them." She laid the three swaddled infants on the bed before Dana. She spoke in Romani, blessing each child as she rubbed some oil onto their little foreheads. Rhys, who already showed his father's temperament, made a disgruntled noise. She laid three amulets into Dana's hand. "Place these over their cribs."

She stayed for a bit, loving on the babies and telling them just how best to make their father crazy, making sure Dana had eaten. Cyrus assumed at the orders or the head chef Cherry and her assistant Reese who had sent up more food than Cyrus could imagine anyone could eat. Seven turkey sandwiches with cranberries had been devoured with no hesitation by the new mother.

"I'll have a few more sandwiches sent down."

"A good idea." Rekkus took the empty plate and handed it to Myron before climbing in the bed next to Dana.

Cyrus looked around the room. Everyone left except Rekkus, Dana, and the babies. He hated to leave, but the time had come. He would use the excuse to bring more food down to come back. Besides, they might need extra hands through the night. "I'll give you some peace."

"Stay, please." Dana halted him as he moved to place the baby beside her. "We need you. Both

Rekkus and I are exhausted, and we love everyone here, but you we trust above all others."

He didn't know if the words were spoken for her or because she understood he needed to hear them, but they were a balm for his soul.

Rekkus slept like a kitten beside the mother of his cubs. Cubs who hadn't shifted yet. Serena agreed to come over throughout the night to sing to the babies to ensure it. Perhaps tomorrow they could make their first shift when mama's strength returned, but for tonight she worked on breastfeeding baby A, while baby B slept in a peaceful milk coma on his daddy's chest, and he got time with the pink-swaddled baby C.

How did you express the joy of touching someone and something so full of innocence and peace? Even when the babies cried, they did so out of necessity and not pain. When Dana suggested he lay the baby skin to skin, his heart melted. Glancing over at her, he could see her fading. Could he protect for her what she held dear because, in all this world outside Rekkus, she trusted only Cyrus.

He felt...honored.

"Can you bring me my glass of ginger ale?" Dana asked, close to falling asleep, careful not to wake Rekkus, or the two slumbering dark-haired identical twins.

Of course he smiled and moved around the bed to the side table. As his bare fingers touched the metal filigree decorating the glass, pain as he never experienced ripped through him as he fought to remain standing. He failed, going to his knees as he clung to Kalina still in his arms. Rekkus leaped out of the bed with an instinct of a father, cradling one child while reaching for the one Cyrus struggled to hold on to. In a second, Dana had all three babies safe in her embrace while Rekkus pulled his friend to his feet.

"Oh my god." Dana, concerned but held in place by her young, asked, "Are you okay?"

"How did you endure it?"

Cyrus was unable to let go of the item, he read, and Rekkus had to pry the cup from his hands. He couldn't catch his breath as the pain Dana had suffered during childbirth racked through him. Her fear, not of the pain, but insecurities she couldn't do it, she couldn't make it, and she wasn't strong enough. Doubts overrode her need to birth her babies. Fear of letting them all down. Then the overwhelming ripping pain of a contraction all over again, followed by sheer exhaustion. The endless grueling cycle showed no signs of ending.

Dana's tears ran down her cheeks as she reached for him. "Touch me."

"It doesn't work like that. It has to be an item." Rekkus spoke for Cyrus when it became obvious he could not.

She grabbed his hand, lifting it to the hemp necklace she wore around her neck, a simple yet beautiful design with three stones in it, one for each baby. "Rekkus made this for me out of love. He placed it on my neck as they handed me Rhys. Touch this."

"You know my pain already," Rekkus encouraged.

Cyrus did know Rekkus' pain as well as experienced it in ways Rekkus hadn't seen. He had been asked by the Syndicate to discover the truth of the black tiger streak massacre. He had seen it all. The pain, the hatred, the insanity. But he told the

Syndicate one simple truth. Rekkus' mom had gone insane and taken out the streak. The rest, no one, not even Rekkus, needed to bear.

"And mine." She indicated the glass.

He reached up, hesitant to touch anything of hers without his gloves. But when he clutched the necklace, it overwhelmed him again, this time not from pain but love. Love far stronger than he could have imagined. First, a wave of Rekkus' love for his mate, not simply the sexual desire—though he experienced that, too—but a soul's burning need to be with her and a selfless affection to put her before his every need. Then Dana's love for Rekkus, deep and complex, a mother's care so strong she could endure anything and would all over again. And joy no one person could contain. Finally, the pain was all but forgotten.

Pulling back, he smiled a real smile not one he forced to ease his family, but real joy. "Thank you."

Dana leaned forward and kissed his forehead. "No, thank you. For, without your need to help others, I never would not have found my family."

"Get some sleep, you two." He wasn't sure how he would manage three babies, but as Rekkus laid back on his side, pulling Dana into his body, she pulled two of the babies into her embrace. He didn't have to ask or be told. He grabbed the baby who lay wide awake. "Rhys Cyrus Duteigr, it's time for me to tell you all about life here on this island."

The baby looked up, wide golden eyes staring at him, and as the baby's little hand wrapped around one of Cyrus' fingers, something in his heart eased. Perhaps the time had come to live again. And he had three little ones to help him relearn how to do it.

About the Author

Award-winning author Dominique Eastwick grew up
a US Navy Brat, so if there was a naval base, that was
probably home. She currently resides in North
Carolina with her husband, two children, crazy lab
and lazy cat.

Dominique's love of reading started when she was
told to read *To Kill a Mockingbird* in high school. A
book that opened her eyes to the joys of reading and
entering into the world of the author. To this day she
ranks this book as her favorite.

Stay connected with my Newsletter:

http://eepurl.com/brjq6D

Also by Dominique Eastwick

Strawberry Kisses
The Duke and the Virgin
The Marquis and the Mistress
The Earl and His Virgin Countess
Infiltrating Her Pack
Shifting Hearts
Siren's Serenade